Bose Creative Publishers (BCP):

A collaborative publishing platform for writers, artists, poets, and changemakers. Profits from book sales support social causes. Books are available as e-books and hardcopies in various online stores. Read more about our books, and our volunteers, in our website.

WWW.BOSECREATIVEPUBLISHERS.CH
Social media: @bosecreativepublishers

Book Layout © 2017 BookDesignTemplates.com
ISBN 978-3-907328-20-0

SHE Authors:

A forum with 30+ women of Indian origin from around the world, from diverse professions, who have come together to write and give a creative platform to the female voice as well as to the underprivileged, and various other narrations from the contemporary world. Books published include: *She Speaks* (short stories, 2018), *She Reflects* (Flash Fiction, 2021), *She Celebrates* (short stories based on Indian festivals, 2021), *Emotions in Rhythm* (poems, 2021), and *She Shines* (short stories, 2022).

Facebook Page: @SHE.Writings

Instagram: @she_writingsbyindianwomen

Youtube: http://bit.ly/SHE-Writings

SHE
in the real and the surreal
...

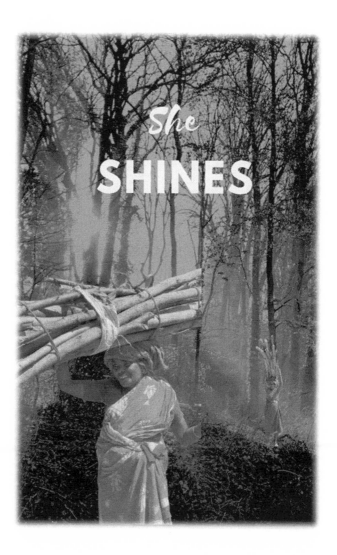

Preface

'She Shines' is the fourth book in the 'SHE' series of books - published as a collaborative project by a group of twenty plus women authors of Indian origin, spread across the world. Hailing from different professional backgrounds, the SHE project's main aim is to provide a creative platform for women's voices and their reflections from daily lives. None of the authors come from a 'purely' literary background - and yet, as scientists, bankers, professors, engineers, managers and home-makers, they all have a story to share.

This creative endeavour started with 'She Speaks' in 2019 (short stories collection) and was followed by 'She Celebrates' in 2020 (reprinted and relaunched in 2021, short stories based on Indian festivals), 'She Reflects' in 2021, (flash fiction stories) and this book 'She Shines' in 2022, which is yet again a short story collection, thereby continuing the theme of highlighting the female perspective.

The stories in 'She Shines' are like myriad precious stones in a necklace - strung together through a common thread, yet each stone has a shape and colour of its own. This common thread is resilience. The victory of darkness over light has been forever a part of the human experience. The female gender throughout cultures, and perhaps through her own unique feminine stance, has borne the brunt of many impossible circumstances. Yet, within her, a certain perseverance and forbearance exists, that can turn things around. The luminosity of light is appreciated because of the darkness surrounding it. It is this simple yet undeniable fact that threads through the stories in 'She Shines'.

Our stories of resilience and victory are seasoned with two different flavours - the real and the surreal. For it is not just the real aspects of our daily lives that lend us an opportunity to win over challenges. But sometimes, the surreal aspect of the human experience may open one's heart to a larger reality than ourselves.

The authors in this book have brought either or both of these aspects to their tales. When reading these stories, you will find a myriad spectrum. Tales of hope, determination, optimism, self-realization and faith raise their heads resolutely amidst geopolitical strife, illegal practices, unchartered territories, personal monsters, and everyday routines. Many are intermixed with surreal realms that defy conventional explanation. This book intends to give voice to the voiceless, bring hidden narrations of the happenings around us into limelight, and bring forth to you, dear readers - stories of a multitude of voices in the shadows.

A unique feature of these stories is that they are based on true events or have been inspired by actual happenings. These stories are compelling because all of us can relate to them in some form.

These are tales about: the joy of friendship and camaraderie amidst dire straits (*Rosita's Birthday*); the trials and tribulations that come with being a refugee and the triumph of building a new life through dogged human determination (*My Day in the Sun; The Little Girl from Barisal*); the will to survive, with it's sweet rewards from the Universe, through it's secret conspiracies and mysterious ways (*A Change of Heart*), or through the warrior goddess dwelling within each one of us (*Lion Heart*); the spark of curiosity lit by paranormal mystery (*Magical Mysteries*); perseverance and personal victory despite horrifying tragedy (*Back from the Dead*); our interconnectedness, eliciting compassion for another's plight and gratitude for little blessings (*Lost Voices*); the natural generosity and faith blossoming in our hearts through the ebbs and tides of life (*The Tale of the Traveling Talisman*); finding one's true self through the shadows of fear and doubt, and standing in one's own light, at last (*Confidente*); turning things around, despite great odds, through the fierceness of spirit (*Just Another Day; Phula*); sheer miracle of motherhood occurring in the face of grief and loss (*The Miracle Child*), and birthing ourselves and another with hope, through the providence of motherhood (*Ndi, Umunyarwandan*).

We hope, dear reader, that your discerning eye will pick up each of these stories, and examine their unique message with your heart. And that, in doing so, you may come to appreciate as well as celebrate the underlying thread of resilience and victory, strung together by diverse female voices. We would also like you to know that by reading our book you will be supporting our philanthropic effort since the profit from book sales

8

will go to non-profit organizations working for women and children.

As editors, we take this opportunity to thank all authors of 'She Shines' for their commitment to this project, despite the business of daily living, with its never-ending list of duties and responsibilities.

Abhilasha Kumar, Raka Mitra, Rejina Sadhu, and Teesta Ghosh

(Editors, SHE 2022 team)

Acknowledgement

COORDINATORS:

Chief Project Coordinator:
Ekta Sharma, Australia
Coordination assistance:
Jesleen Gill Papneja, US

EDITORS:

Abhilasha Kumar, Switzerland
Raka Mitra, The Netherlands
Rejina Sadhu, Switzerland
Teesta Ghosh, US

PROOFREADING:

Teesta Ghosh, US

ILLUSTRATIONS:

Abhilasha Kumar, Switzerland
Teesta Ghosh, US
Picryl, Canva (public domain resources)

Thank you SHE Team.

Contents

SHE Shines through the Real and the Surreal

Dedication

To those, for whom the struggle continues.

'There are two ways of spreading light: to be the candle or the mirror that reflects it.'

– Edith Wharton.

Rosita's Birthday

Teesta Ghosh, USA

Juanita slowly opened her eyes.

Early morning light bathed the tiny room furnished with pieces of worn-out furniture – a bed, a desk, a dresser and a small gas stove in a corner. The walls were covered with drawings that little Rosita brought home from her pre-school. Juanita considered herself lucky for finding a spot in this townhouse meant for homeless single mothers such as herself. The location was not ideal since the Rosedale neighbourhood, tucked away in the south-eastern corner of The Bronx bore all the signs of urban decay – shuttered businesses, run down tenements and graffiti scarred walls.

'Why am I already tired?' Juanita wondered. Mrs. Perlita's incessant coughing next door, through the night had hardly allowed her much sleep. She looked at Rosita sleeping blissfully through it all. Then the next thought that hit her with full force was it was May 2, Rosita's birthday.

She stretched her hand and picked up a blue tin box painted with yellow sunflowers from the desk. She called this box her *El Banco* where she stashed away ones and fives saved from her wages from a part time job in her college's bookstore. For the past six months she had been saving assiduously to celebrate Rosita's birthday. The $110 she had saved had vaporised like raindrops hitting hot asphalt when she had to take her laptop for emergency repairs just prior to her mid-term exams. Juanita opened the *El Banco* and turned it upside down. She was hoping that magically a sum of $55.84 would materialise somehow – precisely the amount she needed for the birthday celebration. A few nickels and dimes tumbled out of the box.

'Wake up *Chiquita*!' Juanita knelt beside Rosita's bed running her hand through her thick brown tresses.

16

'Today is a *mucho mucho* special day. Do you know why?' Those words had a galvanising effect on the five-year-old. Rosita's eyes flew open, and she said, 'It's my birthday Mama! Isn't it?' It was both a question and a statement.

'Yes, it is! Happy birthday my precious,' Juanita said, kissing her daughter's upturned face.

There was no time for a relaxed mother-daughter conversation though. The chiming alarm clock was insistently reminding them that they had only forty minutes before they would have to leave for college and pre-school. Juanita ushered Rosita towards the shared bathroom in the hallway for a quick wash. Rosita was chattering away as Juanita multitasked – pouring a bowl of cereal in a chipped ceramic bowl, stuffing her computer in her backpack and fixing a butterfly shaped barrette on Rosita's hair.

'How old am I today, Mama?' Rosita had asked her for the umpteenth time.

'You are five – Rosie.'

'I am a big girl now Mama, right? When can I go to college like you?'

The doorman, Mr. Corazano, an ageing man with a gentle smile, was leaning against the glass door with the peeling gold lettering that read: New Leaf Shelter. He doffed his cap at Rosita with exaggerated formality. 'Good morning! Miss Rosita Suarez.'

'Hi Mr. Corazano! It's my birthday today and I am going to Dolce Cupcakes in the evening. My Mama said so.' Rosita announced.

'Happy Birthday! How old are you today?'

Rosita raised her hand and spread out her five digits. Juanita and Mr. Corazano exchanged smiles as Juanita hurried Rosita out of the door.

Juanita and Rosita walked quickly, sidestepping construction, traffic and residents who were already on the go. Rosedale was a solid working-class immigrant neighbourhood whose denizens worked as sanitation workers, restaurant servers, taxi drivers and security guards in the swankier boroughs of New York City. A tabby was sunning itself in front of the neighbourhood Bodega which was crowded with early customers.

'Kitty! Kitty!' Rosita slowed to greet the cat.

'Let's go Rosita, otherwise I'll miss my train.' Juanita said impatiently.

Her daily commute to Slomanson College was tightly choreographed. She had to catch the 8:30, to connect to the 9:05 at 96th West which made it possible for her to arrive just in time for the first class of the day at 9:30 AM. The train was crammed, and Juanita wriggled herself to the back of the car where she was lucky to find an empty seat. She sat down and exhaled softly. The day was shaping up to be a busy one. A Math, Computer Science and a Writing Class would keep her on her toes until 3:30 PM. And to top it all she had to finish up a project for Comp Sci and turn it in before the 4 PM deadline.

However, what preoccupied her right then were not pressing academic matters but how she was going to find $55.84 that she needed for Rosita's birthday celebration.

The birthday gift—a rainbow colored xylophone from Target—a birthday card, gift wrapping paper and a balloon would amount to $23.15. A Happy Meal for Rosita and a sandwich for herself at McDonald's was $11.48.

The high point of the evening was going to be a visit to Dolce Cupcakes. Dolce Cupcakes had become an overnight success the moment it opened its doors in the gentrified north-eastern section of The Bronx. The glass fronted store with its candy pink striped awning and melt in the mouth cupcakes attracted a long line of customers. The place drew Rosita like a magnet. She would beg her mother for a cupcake from the store when they passed it on her way back from her preschool. Juanita would have to drag her away because gourmet cupcakes were a luxury that was simply out of reach. Juanita had promised to take Rosita to Dolce Cupcakes for a special birthday treat. She would let Rosita pick five cupcakes from their assorted collection of delectable offerings. This indulgence would bring the total to $55.84.

Juanita mulled over her options in her mind. If she had possessed a credit card, she would have simply charged the amount and worried about paying later. But the fact of the matter was that as a poor student who subsisted on hourly wages, she did not qualify for one.

She could, of course, borrow the money from her affluent friends, fellow students at college who would willingly give her $55.84 and some more if Juanita simply asked. But was Juanita ready to do that? Her group of *amigas*—Stella, Laila, Joshua and Richard knew a Juanita who bore little resemblance to the real one. Juanita Suarez – the college student was bright, funny and an absolute whiz with numbers. When she stepped on the college campus though, she concealed the single homeless mother under a cloak of anonymity. Juanita was afraid that she would be judged by her friends who inhabited the world of high-end sneakers, Apple watches and Beat headphones. Nobody knew except her transgen friend 'Jazz' - Jazmine Romero. Both were kindred spirits united by a common struggle against poverty and prejudice.

The PA system announced her stop – 'the station is 96th West.' Juanita joined the commuters moving towards the exit. The man ahead of her was dragging an enormous suitcase on wheels behind him. The sight of his hirsute wrist with a gold watch clasped on it instantly reminded her of Chico Rodriguez, the Bodega owner in her neighbourhood. Suddenly a solution to her predicament presented itself, however, she also knew that the so-called 'solution' was fraught with perils.

The Bodega was the go-to place for sundry items like bread, milk, detergent, lotto tickets and cigarettes for the neighbourhood's residents. No one knew of Chico's exact origin or when he had showed up in the neighbourhood. He was also a lender from whom the members of the community borrowed during financial

20

emergencies. Rumours were rife about him. There were whispers that he had served jail time for extortion and that he ran a prostitution ring.

Juanita could not avoid the Bodega simply because the nearest grocery store was ten blocks away. There was another reason why she frequented the Bodega anyway. It was comforting to be among Spanish speaking residents who shopped for *frijoles, ancho chilies* and *queso* just like she did.

A particular incident that happened one Saturday afternoon made her suddenly wary of Chico Rodriguez. She was trying to reach for her packet of favorite *Churritos* perched on top of a shelf when Chico appeared by her side. 'Let me help,' he had said. As he reached for the *Churritos* he had brushed against her, and his elbow had touched her breast. She had sprung back reflexively. It had happened so quickly that it left her confused regarding whether his contact with her was accidental or deliberate. Juanita had scrupulously avoided the Bodega for the next few weeks but was forced to go back when she found that she was out of milk for Rosita late one night. After the incident, he was solicitous of her in a way that made her uncomfortable. She knew that Chico would be more than willing to lend her the money, but she was aware that once he sensed her vulnerability she would fall into his trap.

The day dragged on at glacial pace once she was in college. Generally, an attentive student, Juanita had failed to answer a basic question on statistical regressions that the Professor had posed to her. Her mind was elsewhere today. The same question swirled in her mind

21

repeatedly. *Should she get that loan from Chico or break the news to Rosita that her birthday celebrations were cancelled?* It was the last class of the day. As soon as she sat down, Jazz slid into the seat next to her. 'Hey girl! What's up?' Jazz was in her usual ebullient mood. 'May I take you out to Claridges for a meal today?' Claridges was an inside joke between them and referred to a community Church that served free meals to the homeless on Thursdays. 'Can't. It's Rosita's birthday today.' Juanita's curt tone took Jazz by surprise. By then Professor Morrison had put up the first slide on the screen which terminated the conversation between them.

As soon as the class ended, Juanita gathered her belongings and made a beeline for the door. Jazz stared at Juanita's retreating figure puzzled. She followed her and caught up with her near the elevator.

'What's the matter Juani?'

'Why are you avoiding me?

'It's nothing to do with you. I am not in a good mood.

'Tell me about it.'

'I urgently need $55.84 for Rosita's birthday.'

'I had promised her a treat at Dolce Cupcakes. Do you have that money to loan me Jazz? I bet not.'

Jazz knew that Juanita had voiced an unpleasant truth. None of them, both financially strapped students,

22

had the ability to produce an extra dollar, let alone $56 – an extravagant sum.

'I can always ask our friends for a temporary loan.' Jazz was referring to Laila, Joshua, Stella and Richard.

'I absolutely forbid it,' was Juanita's firm command.

'What are you going to do then?'

'I am thinking of going to Chico.' Juanita found a certain relief in verbalizing her decision.

'No! Do not even think of it Juani. It would be a stupid stupid mistake.' Jazz was utterly horrified that her friend was contemplating going to this vile individual.

'I don't see an option here. That's what folks like us have always done when they needed cash. I am not going to break Rosita's heart. You will never understand…'

The last comment was an unkind one and Juanita knew that she had wounded her friend. Jazz was the only one she trusted to look after Rosita when she was sick, and Juanita had to go to work or for her classes. And Rosita was inordinately attached to this overly made up, flashy personality who wore high heels and purple nail polish.

Juanita checked her watch at the station. She was going to pick up Rosita at 5 PM and then head

23

straight to the Bodega. After deciding to go to Chico she suddenly felt very defeated. Her journey from a small town in Texas where she was raised by her *Abuela* to this hard-edged city in search of a better life had squeezed every ounce of energy from the depths of her being.

She had become pregnant in the final year of high school. Her beau, Julio, a star athlete and she had dreams of escaping small town poverty and making it big. The dream died when Julio was killed by a stray bullet while returning from his restaurant job late one night. Juanita's escape from her surroundings had come in the form of a scholarship from Slomanson College in New York City. She had moved to the East Coast with Rosita, determined to write a new chapter for themselves. Her goal of achieving financial security was within grasp. She was going to graduate from college in one more year. On days like this, however, she felt some invisible force was constantly moving the proverbial goal posts.

Rosita was smiling happily when Juanita stopped at the pre-school to pick her up. She tugged at Juanita's shirt excitedly. 'Look Mama, Miss Samantha gave it to me.' Rosita was pointing to a sticker on her dress that said, 'Birthday Girl.'

'Let's get going honey.' Juanita grasped Rosita's hand.

The sky was tinted pale crimson, as mother and daughter stepped on the sidewalk.

'We will go to Dolce Cupcakes once we get home. Right Mama?'

'Yes, darling but first we have to stop at Mr. Chico's to buy cereal for tomorrow's breakfast.'

The Bodega was half empty, when Juanita and Rosita stepped inside it. From the corner of her eye, she could see Chico engaged in animated conversation with the delivery man. Juanita walked over to the shelf of cereal boxes and pretended to examine them. Although her back was turned to him, she felt that he was reading her mind. It seemed Rosita and she were caught in the crosshairs of his predatory gaze and there was no escape. It suddenly felt very cold and unsafe inside the store. Juanita picked up Rosita and ran out of the Bodega.

She was gasping for air and beads of sweat glistened on her forehead when she entered 'New Leaf.' Mr. Corazano was startled to see Juanita in such a state of panic. 'Are you alright Juanita?' His voice was edged with concern. 'Your friends are waiting for you in the lobby.' Juanita had no idea what Mr. Corazano was referring to.

Juanita wheeled around to be greeted by an amazing scene. The lobby was decorated with multicoloured streamers, a humongous red balloon danced gaily in the air and a silver banner said: Happy 5th Rosita! Stella, Laila, Jason, Richard and Jazz were standing and beaming at the two of them. 'Surprise!' they shouted in unison. A large pink box with Dolce Cupcakes emblazoned on it sat on the table.

The look of sheer delight on Rosita's face was priceless. 'It's my birthday party Mama!'

'Well, you are a lucky girl, Rosita. You have many friends who love you dearly.'

Juanita mouthed a silent thank you to Jazz. She was taken aback by the warmth and generosity of her friends.

'Come on, let's get the party going Rosita!' Jazz was unstoppable.

Then Stella picked up her guitar and started strumming and very soon everybody - Rosita, Jazz, Juanita, Laila, Jason, Richard and Mr Corazano were singing and swaying to the beat of 'Baby Shark'. Rosita's birthday party was now in full swing.

Glossary:

Bodega: A Bodega is a convenience store which is to be found in many places all over New York City.

El Banco: The Bank.

Chiquita: A term of affection meaning very little.

Mucho: much or very.

Frijoles: Beans.

Ancho Chilies: A type of chili used in Latin cooking.

Queso:Cheese.

Churritos: A snack made of fried flour.

Abuela: Grandmother.

My Day in the Sun

Saleha Singh, Australia

My eyes are searching for my family, but I'm blinded by the camera and mobile flashes going off in the crowded auditorium. My tears, coupled with my thousand-watt smile, are wiping off the make-up I had so

27

painstakingly applied earlier this morning. But I don't care because today is the most beautiful day of my life.

The certificate that I'm holding so tightly, says I'm a qualified lawyer, and tomorrow, I will join the Human Rights Commission as a Graduate. Yes, my day in the sun is ultimately here.

....

I am Ameena and I was born in Kabul. My earliest memories are of when I was about six. I remember our big house with many rooms and the garden with cherry, apricot, and almond trees. I would spend hours playing and running around the trees with my siblings, Fatima and Majid.

Padar Jaan was an important government officer and Ada taught at the local school—you could call us upper-middle-class. My parents doted on us: we were a happy family who ate, laughed, and enjoyed being together.

I was about 10 when our lives changed irrevocably. I still remember that day—a day like any other when I was returning from school with Fatima, Majid and a few friends.

As we trudged along with our school bags, a group of turbaned men with guns surrounded us. One of them took out his gun.

Right then I heard a loud noise and saw a spark of light followed by smoke. Dust was everywhere, and at the very next moment, Majid and a couple of my friends fell into a heap. I was too shocked to scream, so I ran towards my brother; blood oozed out of his chest as Majid lay unmoving. I called his name, shaking him vigorously, but nothing happened. I don't know for how long I sat there on the road cradling Majid, but my next memory was waking up in a hospital bed.

My hospital stay is very blurry, but when I returned home, everything had changed.

There was an air of heavy sadness that surrounded us.

My parents stopped talking, we stopped going to school, and we didn't play in the garden anymore. Just like that our world had turned upside down. I had nightmares of those gunshots, of me crying out for Majid, but not finding him anywhere.

Padar Jaan returned from work one day and said, 'We're going to Australia soon, so be ready to leave with only your clothes.'

'Why,' I asked.
'Because we can't stay in this country anymore. It's too unsafe,' Padar Jaan replied. 'And Australia is a beautiful country.'

Over the next few months, Ada bought us books about Australia. Fatima and I were very excited. We laughed at the names of cities, were amazed at the pictures of beaches and mountains, and the tall buildings inhaling everything with wonder.

The time to leave came too quickly—I didn't have time to say goodbye to my friends and somehow, I knew that I wouldn't see them again. But the momentary sadness was replaced by the excitement of flying. I had never been on an aeroplane before, so being up in the clouds and touching the sky was indeed novel.

After two days of changing flights, we reached Jakarta.

'Is Jakarta in Australia?' I asked Padar Jaan.
'No, we will take another flight to Australia,' he replied. 'We will take a bus to Cisarua, stay there for a few days, and then go to Melbourne. You will like the place, trust me.'

We shared a house overlooking the mountains with three other families, who were just like us—going to Australia. Sharing a house with others was a first for us—it was too crowded.

I don't remember much of our days in Cisarua. Maybe, those memories have become blurred. Four couples shared the house with us. Fatima and I would take out the books Ada had bought us, and read about Australia and entertain ourselves, imagining what it would be like to live there. Ada and Padar Jaan would talk in whispers, most of which we couldn't catch.

Every few days, Padar Jaan would make a three-hour bus journey to the United Nations High Commission for Refugees in Jakarta and return late at night. Silently, he would shake his head, and in time, we understood that moving to Australia wasn't going to be easy. The initial euphoria gave way to resignation and despondency.

We must have stayed in Cisarua for about 18 months when, one day, Padar Jaan said that we were leaving for Australia. I was filled with exhilaration, excited about the Australian cities, the beaches, and the tall buildings that we, so longingly, were looking forward to.

We packed our four suitcases—our only belongings—and traveled in a truck with 40 – 50 people. We walked through thick, jungle foliage, the road leading to a steep hill before arriving at the water's edge where nearly 100 people had gathered. Fatima and I were tired, hungry, and thirsty, but Ada shushed us. Late into the night, we boarded a boat—packed like sardines.

That five-day, tumultuous journey is etched in my mind forever. We sat crouched, squeezed between unknown bodies—smelling each other's sweat, fear, and breath, with babies screaming—sailing through the choppy waters of the Indian Ocean, all for a better life ahead. As we neared Australia, we were intercepted by an Australian Navy boat. We were asked to show our papers while being unceremoniously dumped into their boat and ferried to an island. Little did I know then that this was going to be our home for the next three years.

I grew up during the time we spent at the Christmas Island Detention Centre. While Ada, Fatima, and I shared a tiny room with a bed, Padar Jaan was put in the adjoining men's facility. We were not criminals but were treated as such. We were made to do heavy, manual work around the facility, which we weren't equipped to

31

do. There were two bathrooms for women, but only women with children could use them. Ada would take Fatima and me for a shower and catch one herself. Many single women borrowed children from other mothers. During the early years, Fatima and I soiled ourselves many times, before Ada woke us up at the crack of dawn so that we could use the toilet. The ignominy of those days is etched clearly in my mind—the shame and embarrassment of it all.

For the first time, I saw men propositioning women for sexual favours and my teenage mind was shocked. Each day was a revelation—caged within barbed wire fencing—with nothing to look forward to.

I saw women suffer from serious mental health issues, as they couldn't see light at the end of the tunnel. Some tried to kill themselves by drinking detergent or putting plastic bags around their heads; others slit their wrists, while some tried unsuccessfully to hang themselves. Initially, I would cry but as days melted into weeks, and weeks into months, and months into years, I promised myself that when I got out of detention—and I was sure we would—I would become a lawyer. I would be the voice for these hundreds of voiceless women.

Every few months, officials would come and talk to Ada, Fatima, and me about why we left Kabul. Sometimes Padar Jaan would join us. And every time we saw him, he looked frail with a vacant resigned look in his eyes.

We were in detention for around three years when we were asked to meet the officials yet again.

The news stunned us—we were on a bridging visa and moving to Melbourne.

We were now refugees.

This news wasn't as exciting to me as I had initially expected. I had changed so much.

We were settled in a predominantly Caucasian suburb in Melbourne. We now lived in a house with separate rooms and a bathroom for ourselves—a luxury. I had lost so many years of my life and was keen to go back to school. I was already 16 years old and had fallen behind my peers in education. For the next two years, Fatima and I went to a special English school, to catch up. We put our heart and souls into our learning, and after two years, were ready for school. Both of us were the oldest students when we enrolled in Year 9.

Mistakenly, we had thought our detention days were behind us. We were bullied incessantly. Some students laughed at our accents, made fun of our hijabs and skin colour. After our years in detention, nothing could deter us—we were in for the long haul and knew we had to make a life for our family.

I had made up my mind to study Law and quickly realised that to get there, I needed extraordinarily good marks. Fatima wanted to be a doctor, specialising in psychiatry.

Our years in detention had shaped our future.

33

While Fatima and I started dreaming of our future, Padar Jaan was going downhill. Although allowed to work, he couldn't find employment and each rejection brought him to the brink of a breakdown.

Meanwhile, Ada started cleaning houses as she couldn't get any other job. Like most Australian teenagers, Fatima and I worked various jobs to help with household expenses and kept little for pocket money.

Being on the brink of poverty was normal for us—life in Kabul was long forgotten.

We graduated from high school with high scores when I was 22.

A university scholarship followed; for the next few years, I had to forego social outings and put my heart into my studies.

I applied to multiple law firms for voluntary jobs and apprenticeships and was accepted as a paralegal at a law firm working with refugee women.

Those were the best years of my life, albeit the occasional mockery I faced on the streets about my hijab, being spat at, and told to go back where I came from.

My university results were not unexpected. I had worked hard, and most days when I came back home, I was exhausted, juggling classes, university assignments, and a job. But I pursued my goal single-mindedly, despite not being able to go out for a meal, to the beaches, or discover the beautiful city of Melbourne. I knew my day in the sun would come.

....

I wake up to a bright sunny morning—so unusual for Melbourne winters.

I can't help the flutter of excitement in my stomach. I turn to see the smiling faces of Padar Jaan, Ada, and Fatima.

Tears roll down Padar Jaan's face—this time, it's not the depression that makes him cry, but pride and happiness.

He holds up a piece of paper and I quickly scan the contents.

We are now permanent residents—after 10 years of living in Australia, we now have a country which we can call our own. There's no more fear of being sent back to where we came from.

I don't believe in miracles; nothing has come easy in our lives.

But is this a harbinger of better days and my graduation day is just the beginning?

Fatima still has a year to complete her degree, but we know she's as committed as me. We've both been each other's support when things have crumbled around us.

I dress quickly, apply perfect make-up, and wear my new dress—a rare splurge—with my favourite yellow hijab.

My family will meet me at the university auditorium in a few hours.

My graduation gown complements my hijab and I'm ready when my name is called. I walk to the stage to receive my graduation certificate—I'm officially a lawyer today.

My eyes are searching for my family, but I'm blinded by the camera, and mobile flashes going off in the crowded auditorium. Yes, my day in the sun is finally here!

Epilogue: This story is based on true events.

Glossary:

Ada: mother
Padar Jaan: father

A Change of Heart

Abhilasha Kumar, Switzerland

A piece of Danny's spirit had escaped dissolution. His healthy heart, recently separated from the body it had occupied for eighteen years, now swam in a liquid buffer, connected to electric tubes and electrodes.

Not far from where Danny's heart was inwardly dreaming and outwardly beating in a deep jar, Paula's limp body lay in deep, anaesthesia-induced sleep. Pale and desperately in need now, the once-feisty Paula was dying of a failing heart. There wasn't much left in her, except a will to live, that was holding her tenuously onto this life.

Her debilitating heart disease meant that by the time she was sixteen, Paula had to be enlisted for a heart transplant. She had to wait two years to the day, to get a chance to extend her life.

Her overwhelmed mother had quietly broken the news to Paula that the hospital had found a matched donor. Everyone in the family had breathed a sigh of relief but were understandably worried about the outcome of this major surgery. *A matched donor is a marriage made in heaven, but any marriage can go wrong.*

It had all happened too quickly for Paula to be sufficiently nervous. Just before she was wheeled into the operation theatre, an involuntary, deep exhalation had dispelled any lingering fear; in that moment of surrender, it had felt right for her to trust the process. When she woke after the transplant, groggy with anaesthesia, with pain stronger than the morphine working through her veins, paralyzed by hundreds of tubes traversing in and out of her, eighteen-year-old Paula already felt different. She had a good feeling about this. She knew she was going to live. The sounds from her new heart felt like that of a tiny dancer, foot-tapping rhythmically on the dance floor. It was a new beat, a new rhythm, a new life.

Paula recovered more quickly than doctors had expected. Whereas they attributed her quick healing to her youth and the condition of her donor's heart, Paula attributed it to the Universe, to something unnameable and omniscient, that she felt was looking out for her.

Once back in her house, stripped free of tubes and monitors, Paula began to settle into her new life. In the silence of her room, it was easier to hear the rhythmic beating of her new heart. In the quietude of night-time, it felt like someone else was present with her. It was a strange sensation at first. Fine tuning herself to perceive extra-sensorial reality was like hearing with light and seeing with sound. Sometimes, it felt like a waft of perfume bearing a message had been carried into the room by the wind. After it trailed away, disappearing into the air, she would wonder - *did it happen at all?* It seemed surreal at first. But with patience and practice, the faint feelings born in her new heart became stronger by the day. And so, Paula, started to enjoy her new life -getting robust by day, listening to her heart's inner music by night.

She gradually became aware that there was a boy around her, who seemed to know who she was. He was ever present with her. With her growing awareness of his presence, she felt uneasy about unzipping her jeans to go to the toilet or undressing. He felt so intimate, like a lover. She couldn't tell anyone about this disembodied friend. However, over the months, she grew used to feeling his presence. In this newfound company, she

39

started feeling comfortable and would talk about everything - share about the day and its most mundane happenings, and bare her innermost longings.

Paula's family saw that their wild, hot-tempered daughter had become quieter and calmer after her surgery, albeit with a stronger body now. The colour had returned to her pale skin. She had more energy than before and went back to her final school year, did her homework, and spent many hours in her room, humming to herself. One day, Paula said, 'Mom, I want to learn to play the guitar.' 'I thought you liked hip-hop,' her mother commented, rhetorically. 'That was back then. I just really love the sound of the acoustic guitar now. I think I'll take some lessons,' quipped Paula.

At times, Paula heard a faint tune, as if it were floating in from a distance. At other times, it felt like someone was singing to her. *Could it be real?* She was almost reluctant to admit it, but it definitely felt like she was being serenaded. A tune came to her each day, although its lyrics were just out of the reaches of her mind. The words of the song were undecipherable, but the guitar notes were discernible, as if it had travelled from afar, on the wind. Paula started to trust the ways of the wind. The wind whispered music through her gossamer filaments to Paula; she also kept Paula's secret in her airy folds, becoming a trusted confidante.

Music wasn't the only thing that had changed in Paula. She couldn't stand meat anymore. She used to love the beef stew her mother made. Now, the smell of meat cooking in her proximity sent her reeling with nausea. She became a vegetarian.

The girl who had found it difficult to wake up in the morning each day, would now rise at the crack of dawn, and instinct would guide her to light a candle and close her eyes. Under the tutelage of the boy's wispy presence, she learnt to slow her breath, and still her mind. In the pause between breaths and thoughts, which got longer with each session, she experienced something beyond human vocabulary. She found out much later, in her late twenties, that what she was instinctively practicing then, was a meditation technique that people paid money to learn.

Paula's communication with the original owner of her new heart was mostly musical, wordless, and instinctive. It was like driftwood floating on a sea of daily sensory perception – distinct, free, light, and without agenda. One could supposedly assign blame to the rulership of youth's raging hormones, but the truth was that Paula was in love with this boy whom she had never seen. Perhaps his name was whispered by the wind, or perhaps, the name came to her in a flash of inner knowing, for she started calling him Danny.

Her family wasn't surprised when Paula finally declared that she wanted to meet her donor's family. It took some time to cut through the bureaucratic process of California's state department, and get hold of details. They finally had the name and address.

Her heart stopped for a moment, when she saw the name of the donor on the form that was mailed by the hospital. Her donor had been a boy of eighteen; his name was Danny Whitman. His parents lived an hour's drive away from Paula's home.

41

A phone call was exchanged between parents and a meeting was arranged.

She dressed nervously that Sunday morning in the spring of 2000, taking care to wear a knee-length sundress and tidy her brunette locks into a dainty ponytail. 'I am going to meet your parents and see your home, after all,' she told Danny. She hummed that familiar tune once again.

Danny's mother, Mrs Whitman, seemed feeble and frail. His father was tall and stoic. It was clear that they were both still grieving. It had been nearly two years since the car accident. They were equally nervous about meeting the recipient of their son's heart. 'We were looking forward to meeting you, Paula. Thank you for wanting to meet us as well,' said Mrs Whitman with a disarming smile.

'I am alive because of your son. I have a feeling that he was quite special. I would like to honor his memory. And know more about him. What was he like?' Paula asked them. She couldn't keep it in any longer; she had to know about Danny, who had her heart. *Or rather, whose heart she had.*

Paula's composure cracked when she spotted Danny's photograph in the living room. There was, inexplicably, an instant recognition. Her heart – *his heart* – leaped and skipped a beat. She was simultaneously curious and sad, wishing she had known him when he was alive.

Mrs Whitman's eyes lit up faintly as she spoke of Danny. 'He was always the quiet one, our Danny.'

42

'He loved music. Oh yes, he did. By the time he was twelve, he was playing the guitar like a pro. He wrote songs; made up his own tunes.'

'Something strange began to happen when he was that age. He would spend hours alone in his room. He started waking up at dawn. Sometimes, I would come by to see if he was feeling unwell, but no, he would just sit by candlelight with his eyes closed, unaware that I was at the door. We thought it was some weird, new-age culture at school that he was being exposed to. But you know, he was always the meditative, sensitive sort. He was even a vegetarian; he couldn't stand meat,' Mrs Whitman's voice softened, with fond reminiscences.

'That was not nearly as strange as when Danny started talking to us about organ donation. At first, we thought they must be talking about it at school. But then, he came on too strongly. He said he absolutely must do it as soon as possible,' Mrs Whitman's voice broke as she recalled how determined her son had been.

Mr Whitman took over, and continued, while his wife regained her composure. 'As you know, the law doesn't allow children to make this decision. So, on his fourteenth birthday, we had to sign the registry form for organ donation. It seemed rather strange to us, but we had to respect his wishes, because it was clear that he felt very strongly about it. He didn't tell us much else.'

'It was only after he passed that we understood,' Mrs Whitman appeared to have gotten a second wind now. 'We couldn't make ourselves clear out his stuff for a long time. But after last Thanksgiving, we finally mustered up enough courage to do it. In his closet, we

43

found self-recorded CDs of his songs. We found poems so profound and full of knowing, you wouldn't think a teenager had written them. Most peculiarly, he had kept a diary all along. When we read through it, God bless him, we found out that he had known since he was twelve that he was going to die in a road accident and give his heart to someone. He had seen it in his dreams,' she said, her gaze piercing Paula.

Paula felt the hairs at the back of her neck stand up. 'You are welcome to peer through his diaries, poems, and songs. I think he would like that. But there's something we would like for you to hear. It's one of his songs. It all makes sense now, Paula,' said Mrs Whitman, looking at peace for the first time since their meeting.

Mr Whitman left the living room briefly and returned with a CD in his hand. Quietly, he placed it on the CD player.

Paula was familiar with the tune of the guitar. It was the same tune that the wind had taught her; the same one that she often hummed. *He had a soft voice, her Danny.* Those elusive lyrics came to her at last, as Danny's voice filled the room. It felt like the clicking sound of a lock that had been turned by the right key.

Soon enough, it will all come through.

Though a rolling stone,

gathers no moss.

Long enough, I'll keep it for you,

44

whatever it costs.

Paula, my heart is yours!

Paula, my heart is yours!

Paula, my heart is yours!

Epilogue:

This story is inspired by true events.

Paula Silvan changed her name to Paula Whitman when she was twenty-two years of age. She became a successful country music singer, and composed music for all of Danny's poems and songs. Her debut song, 'Danny, my heart is yours,' topped music charts, for several weeks in a row. Paula's heart is still going strong. She continues to compose music and sing to this day and has a close relationship with Mr and Mrs Whitman.

Lionheart

Jesleen Gill Papneja, US

'We have to go! Leave anything that you cannot wear.' Fauja's voice sounded equally emphatic and concerned.

The entire family looked at him in bewilderment. His suggestion meant that they would be leaving behind everything—their home, vast lands, cattle and horses, and all of their wealth.

There had been reports of looting and massacres in neighbouring villages. Homes were being burnt, men mercilessly butchered, and women and children abducted. Now, the mob was dangerously close to their village, and they were expected to attack at dusk tomorrow. Everyone was planning to leave the next morning, at the crack of dawn, to escape the brutality which was ominously close.

Amrit looked at her older brother and then at her ancestral home. She had come across the border to visit her family in Pakpattan. Her family had been very keen to see her younger son whom they had not met before, and who was now four years of age. As her husband, Karam Singh (an officer in the Royal Air Force), would be very busy that summer, Amrit decided to spend a couple of months with her family so that the children could get to spend a little time with them. She had not had contact with Karam for a few weeks and hoped that he was alright.

Fauja's voice broke into her thoughts. He was discussing the details with Amarjot and Babu, his younger brothers. 'Tomorrow morning, we will start walking towards Arifa and then on to Haveli. Jeeta is waiting for us in Jangha and will help us cross the border into Hindustan.'

'We should be able to cross over in a few days. Then we have to start our quest of looking for Karam.'

Amrit looked over at her two sons, running around and playing in the courtyard of her family home, pretty much as she had done as a young girl. Amreek (seven) lifted little Gurtej (four) high into the air, and the little boy squealed with glee. It was getting dark and Amrit wanted the boys to get plenty of rest before the long journey the next day, so she took them in.

Amrit had just drifted into light slumber when Tara, her brother's wife, burst into her room. 'Amrit, get up! Get up now Amrit! The mob is coming, and they will reach us in a matter of minutes. You have to leave now!'

Startled and wide awake now, Amrit could hear screams and wails through the night air. She quickly woke her sons, Amreek and Gurtej, and half dragged them into the courtyard.

Everyone was running around trying to gather and hide what they could. Amrit stood as if rooted to the spot.

Fauja found her and jolted her to reality, 'Amrit there is no time to lose. The mob has struck tonight instead of tomorrow. We all must leave now. You and the children should leave right away. I've prepared a horse for you. Amrit! Can you hear me? There is no time to think, only act! You must ride out to Jangha with Amreek and Gurtej!'

Amrit continued to just stare at Fauja without being able to move. 'How can I take Amreek and Gurtej by myself?' She finally found her voice and looked at her brother helplessly, 'They don't even know how to ride.'

'No, but their mother does. You are the finest rider I know, Amrit. And tonight, you will ride for the sake of your children. You will ride!'

And saying that, Fauja Singh did something that Amrit could never have dreamed of. He removed his turban and called Amreek to stand behind Amrit. He started to strap and secure the boy to Amrit's back with his turban.

His turban!

The crown that he was most proud of! Amrit had never seen her brother without one. Fauja's pride in being a Sikh was represented by his iconic turban, but he never batted an eye when removing it to help his sister. Amrit just stood there as her brother strapped Amreek onto her, her eyes filled with tears of gratitude, for she understood the emotion behind the act.

In an instant, Amarjot, her younger brother, was by their side. He also removed his turban to secure Gurtej to Amrit's front. And then Babu removed his turban, to make a loop that secured the other turbans into place and made a makeshift holster on either side of Amrit. Badal, her horse, was harnessed and waiting for her. The brothers helped Amrit mount and made sure that the children were still securely fastened to her.

Amarjot and Babu packed two loaded rifles into the holsters by Amrit's side and Fauja handed her a sword, chanting, '*Deh siva bar mohe eh-hey subh karman te kabhu na taro, na daro arr seo jab jaye laro nischey kar apni jit karo!*' (Translation: Dear God, grant my request so that I may never deviate from doing good deeds. That, I shall

50

have no fear of the enemy when I go into battle and with determination, I will be victorious).

Amrit's eyes brimmed with tears.

This was the same anthem that the four siblings had sung with their father, and it had been a source of miraculous strength for them. Amrit didn't know if she would ever see any of them again.

As though reading her mind, Fauja said, 'Don't worry about us. We will be fine. You need to get out of here before the mob reaches our village. We are following right behind you.'

With that, he led the horse out of the house and Amrit galloped away into the night.

As Amrit reached the outskirts of her village, she saw an orange glow emanating ahead of her. She sat on her black horse, paralyzed! The fumes and glow from the flaming villages, and the blood-curdling screams of the villagers, either being burnt alive or being pierced by the metal swords, reverberated through the air. Shaking her from her state of numbness, was the rapid and yet reassuring thudding of little heartbeats on her chest and back.

Her sons—her soul! If she had any hopes of saving them and giving them the future that she knew was destined to be theirs, she knew what she had to do – ride through the blazing village of flames and massacre, and get them to the other side—to her people, to safety. She looked down at the sinewy head of her four-year-old son, strapped onto her torso. She turned back and saw

the frightened yet determined profile of her other son –
just seven, but with the heart of a lion, strapped to her
back.

As Gurtej looked up at his mother, his charcoal
black eyes gave her the courage she needed. She gave him
a reassuring smile, adjusted and tightened the straps that
bound her sons to her, and felt for the bulky, reassuring
security of the two rifles secured on either side.

She clutched her trusted sword ever so tightly in
her right hand, and the reins of her horse in her left, and
shouted as loud as her lungs would allow,

'Jo Bole so Nihal.'

Her sons responded with equal fervor, 'Sat Sri
Akal!' and clasped their mother tightly, as she urged her
stallion to charge through the night towards the blazing
village.

Amrit rode through flaming village after flaming
village, oblivious to the sights and the sounds around her.
She rode through the night without stopping once. In the
pale early morning light, she could just about begin to
make out the village of Jangha, coming closer with every
gallop. After riding through the night without a pause, it
was as if Badal had forgotten how to slow down or stop.

He continued to maintain his speed even after
Amrit attempted to slow him down several times. Now
she was afraid that he would ride through Jangha without
stopping. She screamed for anyone to hear. As she got
closer to the village, a mob of people came running
towards her.

52

For a few seconds, Amrit thought that all was lost.

The mob, that she had so stoically ridden away from, had found her and her entire journey had been in vain.

Suddenly, strong hands grasped the reins and saddle, and slowly, Badal came to a halt. Amrit looked down into the welcoming eyes of Jeeta, her uncle, and his friends. They helped Amrit down and unfastened Amreek and Gurtej from their mother.

Relief flooded Amrit and she collapsed, clutching her sons to her, finally having made it to safety.

Author's Note

This is based on a true story. It is very close to my heart as it is the story of my maternal grandmother, who rode through the night on horseback during the time of India and Pakistan's partition in 1947. This story is truly inspiring for me because I believe it to be the reason for my existence. My grandmother showed exceptional courage and made it back to India, in 1947. In 1948, my mother was born. If that day, she had faltered and not shown the mettle she was made of, my mother would never have been born, and by that, nor would I. In that one night, my grandmother defined courage and valor for multiple generations to come. I dedicate this story to my grandmother and all those valiant women who rise above challenges every day, and fight against odds for everything they consider to be true and right!

Magical Mysteries

Ekta Sharma, Australia

Quite often it's the more secluded off-road places that provide food for thought and leave us with long-lasting memories.

Rohini, a writer by profession, was particularly interested in the genre of mystery, suspense, and history, therefore she loved visiting haunted villages and ghost towns. For her, ghost stories held a very different kind of charm.

Through her writings, she wanted to lure her readers to old forts, ruins of castles, deserted alleys, and sinister houses, visited by abandoned spirits. The stories gave her a chance to peep right into the lives of the people who once inhabited them. So, when her husband Ram told her about 'Kuldhara', a haunted ghost village and the legends associated with it, she knew what her next project would be.

Situated 18 km from the Golden City of Jaisalmer in Rajasthan, Kuldhara, a large village had an interesting story to tell. Since the 13th century, Kuldhara had been a bustling settlement of the Paliwal Brahmin community. However, one night in the year 1825, the entire settlement of about 85 villages including Kuldhara was abandoned, it looked as if it was in a hurry, with chores left unfinished in homes.

The village was left with dilapidated mud houses with missing roofs, and all traces of human life gone. Even though the whole village turned sadly into ruins, the Ganesha temple which was right in the middle of the town still stood sturdy and unchanged, after nearly two centuries.

'It would be great to discover the stories of the once-prosperous village. I can figure out how and why people who have tried to stay there have either been

56

chased away, or have simply disappeared due to a strange paranormal phenomenon that occurred there,' Rohini felt.

'Let me do my homework properly before actually visiting the site and writing the article,' she thought.

As she opened her laptop and began reading about the place, all the characters in the various myths and stories that had grown around Kuldhara over the centuries, started appearing in front of her eyes.

The article confirmed that a prosperous settlement of the Paliwal Brahmins had lived there since 1291 and then had mysteriously disappeared.

According to a popularly held notion, the village was now inhabited by ghosts. Some people believed that the unsatiated souls of the inhabitants still roamed all over the village, while others said that there existed a treasure consisting of gold buried under the land, and ghost stories were spread by the locals to keep visitors away from the place.

Another legend was that there was either a scarcity of water or an earthquake that had forced the residents away.

Rohini quickly found out that there existed many intriguing stories which tried to find an explanation for the current state of the village. However, the most famous of these was that the 'haunted' village was abandoned by its inhabitants because of atrocities committed by a powerful ruler of Jaisalmer, Salim Singh.

The residents were pounded with heavy taxes and were treated very inhumanly. The ruler was known for his debauchery and unscrupulous tax-collecting methods. So, the villagers had no alternative, but to vacate overnight and escape from the grasp of the ruler.

Another popular legend mentioned that a former Kshatriya ruler had set his eyes on the beautiful daughter of the village chief, a Paliwal Brahmin, some 200 years back. This was a time when inter-caste marriage was forbidden. It was said that due to the incessant pressure on the Brahmin community, a decision was taken by the residents to teach the King a lesson by deserting the village.

However, no one saw the thousand-odd members of the village leave and for generations now, no one knows where the Paliwals resettled.

When the Paliwals left the villages, they cursed that nobody could ever inhabit the villages. If anyone lived there, they would be cursed with bad luck throughout their life. Residents of Jaisalmer mentioned that despite the curse, there have been some attempts by families to inhabit the place, but they could not succeed.

'The content seems to be interesting and it would be worth paying a visit to the place,' Rohini thought.

'There's bound to be an eerie silence all around it and that should add to the mystique of the place.'

She was getting goosebumps, as she continued to read about Kuldhara.

'Ro,' said Ram lovingly. 'Let's go to Kuldhara tomorrow and watch the sunset and click photos. The ruins would add a scenic backdrop for the photographs.' he pitched humorously.

'What?' Rohini snapped out of her thoughts.

'You do realize it's a haunted site and not a place from where to bring back souvenirs,' stated Rohini, removing her spectacles and looking at her husband's face.

Despite Rohini not being in favour of the idea, the next day the couple started early to reach Kuldhara in time before the gates to the village closed. As they reached the dusty road leading to the town, Rohini noticed that other than them, there were no humans in sight and only minimal vegetation – the meek straying goats that she spotted, had most likely feasted on the last remains.

The afternoon sun was fiery when they reached the ruined gates of the ancient village. Rohini felt that time had stood still for the last 200 years. Intermittent rows of mud houses, narrow lanes, sandstone walls, and a temple stood as a living testimony of some sad past.

To the east of the village was the parched riverbed of Kakni. As Rohini and Ram walked through the ruins of Kuldhara, ravages of time were visible all over. Kuldhara was a desolate place and an uncanny silence prevailed all around.

As a visitor to the abandoned village, Rohini was bound to feel curious about its past. She wanted to learn about how without a trace the locals disappeared and that too, without drawing any attention to their evacuation and more importantly, what happened to them. So many questions were cropping up in her mind. These were questions that her readers and most importantly she wanted answered to settle the turmoil within her.

'So, what story do you know about this place?'

Rohini asked, to the only human present there—the gatekeeper Mohan. 'Please, can you narrate the legend, and the curse?' Rohini asked with a pause.

'There is a curse that for 200 years this village will be barren and uninhabited,' said Mohan.

'This is all because a *Sadhu* came to this village and villagers didn't treat him well. It is believed that as a result, he cursed the land and the villagers. All the villagers were transformed into statues of sand. Later a big storm came which destroyed all the statues. Villagers were dead but their souls still remain in the area,' Mohan said.

'Some people have mentioned they have heard voices during the night coming from the village. Some even said that when they walk, they feel as if someone is behind them or someone has put a hand over their shoulder. But when they turn around, it's only wind and silence that they find,' he added.

'It seems to be true,' replied Rohini pointing at the scant presence of human existence and minimal vegetation.

'See, the houses are in ruins but they have remained the way they were left behind by their inhabitants centuries ago,' added Ram.

As both climbed up the steps of one such home, they could see the entire expanse of the village. Lanes and brick homes, equidistant from each other, were neatly laid out.

'Ram look!' said Rohini excitedly. 'I can spot the Hindu temple, amidst all these ruins.'

'But that does not explain how a cluster of 85 villages was abandoned overnight' questioned Ram. 'Or why as some say the kitchen fire was still on, chores were still being done and just the people vanished. Or why none of the houses were left without roofs after the people disappeared'.

'Interesting,' thought Rohini.

Reports of many strange and unnatural activities that keep on happening at this place have attracted several ghost hunters and intrepid paranormal societies. People from different parts of the world visit Kuldhara to see the dark and spooky side of Rajasthan and try to unveil its mysterious secrets. The events of just one night had made this a godforsaken place for the rest of the centuries.

As the sun started to set across the dunes, Mohan hastily requested the couple to leave. 'The gates of Kuldhara will be closed soon. After 6 pm, no tourists are allowed as we believe that spirits still haunt the village after sunset. You have to go now please,' he continued.

Ram held Rohini's hand as they rushed back.

'Are you ok? How was your experience?' asked Ram.

'Ethereal,' Rohini said after a long pause. 'I have no words. I am feeling a bit uneasy and sad. I'm not quite sure why. But the legend and curse of Kuldhara have left me fascinated,' she added.

'Whatever it was, it is not easy to uproot yourself unless it is due to some anxiety and hardship,' she continued.

'What do you think, Ram?' she asked.

'It was a quiet atmosphere and a welcome relief from the hustle and bustle of Jaisalmer Fort, or the dunes close by,' Ram chuckled. He did not want to add to Rohini's uneasiness.

'By the way, do you know that the Paranormal Society of India heard spooky voices, saw shadows that moved, and found hand-prints of children on cars when their team visited Kuldhara,' mentioned Rohini. 'There seems to be something mysterious going on here,' she added.

The story of Kuldhara was indeed fascinating and shrouded in mystery. Everyone who had read the story or visited the place was left intrigued by it.

Ram, who did not believe in ghosts earlier, was also feeling a sudden chill. Was it because of the eeriness of the place or what Rohini had just mentioned, or was it simply the cool evening breeze of the desert? He was not quite sure. He was forced to acknowledge that many happenings simply cannot be explained by logic or science.

The dark secrets of the desert and ghostly stories will always be there, but above all, the once well-planned settlement left an impression of sadness. One cannot help but ask, 'What went wrong?'

Epilogue:

At present, Kuldhara village is a heritage site and is maintained by the Archaeological Survey of India.

Glossary:

Sadhu: A religious ascetic, mendicant, or any holy person in Hinduism and Jainism who has renounced the worldly life.

Back from the Dead

Savvy Soumya Misra, India

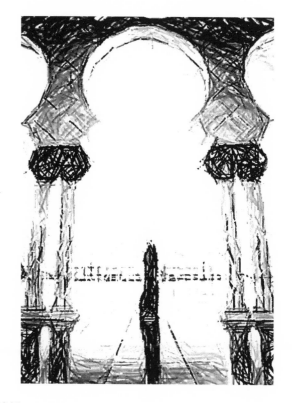

2017

'It's been 17 years and I can still taste the blood.'

2000

He walked in with a stone. A big stone. He was furious at her. She just wanted him to go to work.

It had been less than a day that he had brought her back from her brother's house. Had sex with her. She never once called it making love. She cooked for him. He got her a glass of milk. She had just finished it and she casually asked him about work.

The last thing she remembered was being hit on the head twice (at least), blood on her face, and splattered on the walls. She remembered falling on the ground. She also remembered hearing herself cry for help. But she couldn't have. The heavily pregnant Sultana Begum had passed out.

When she woke up 21 days later, she was in a general ward of a government hospital in Hyderabad. Her head and face were bandaged. Sultana had slipped into a coma that day after the assault. Her neighbours had rushed her to the hospital.

2017

'It was the eighth month of my pregnancy. My child was safe, *Alhamdulillah*! What I didn't know was the full extent of my injuries.'

2000

The police spoke to her. Arrested the husband. They said it was a 'personal matter' between husband and wife. They let him go, as there was no chargesheet.

on her own. When she went back to her family for a few days, she was doled out the usual spiel—A girl goes to her marital home in a *doli*, and should leave only on an *arthi*.

On that day in 2000, she had nearly left on an *arthi*.

2000

The doctors told her it was a complicated case. A surgery was due, and so was her delivery. They didn't want to take any chances. 'You should call someone from your family.'

No one came to meet Sultana at the hospital. No one—neither her three siblings, nor her father, or her sister-in-law—no one.

The doctors offered support if she wanted to file a complaint with the police. She didn't quite think about it. The safe delivery of her child was her only priority.

Twenty-five days after coming out of a coma, she was shifted to a maternity hospital. Once again, she was asked about family.

'I have relatives but no one will come.' She told her entire story. 'All I remember is that I was hit and all I know is that I need my baby to be safe.'

'You have to sign a form. If something happens to you, who should be held responsible?'

'Please write my husband's name. He is responsible for my condition,' came her reply.

Sultana made a final request before being wheeled into the operation theatre. 'Save my child. Save me if possible. I want to talk to the police afterwards.'

Sultana gave birth to a baby boy. Seven days passed, and no one turned up. The doctor spoke to a few reporters. Her story was published in the papers.

2017

'When they heard it was a boy, the family started turning up.' She refused to go with either side of the family. With her surgery due, she was referred back to the general hospital. She stayed there for a month, took care of her child, and got herself treated.

'After a month, my brother came and apologised, and took me home.'

The neighbours went bonkers on her first day in her brother's house.

They called her a bad influence. Instead of backing the woman who was nearly stoned to death, and had her face disfigured beyond repair, they made her the villain of the piece.

They hurled insults in Hindi at her that her own city had cut off her nose to spite her: '*Itni neechi aurat hai ki uskey shehar ne iska naak kaat diya!*'

70

'If she is here, our girls would learn to raise their voice, demand their rights and eventually be beaten up. She can't stay here' they had said. 'They fought with my brother.'

2000

Her brother buckled. She took her baby, walked out of his house, with nowhere to go.

The only place she could think of was the government hospital. She went back, pleaded with the nurses and doctors, who had taken care of her for nearly a couple of months, to let her stay in the hospital. They agreed.

For the next seven months, the government hospital in Hyderabad was her address. She helped out the nurses, and did odd jobs for them. Her son was being taken care of by the faculty there.

2017

'I worked but also faced a lot of ridicule because of my face. I was ragged. People got scared, uncomfortable even. They didn't want to deal with me, they didn't want me near them.'

Sultana has told her story so many times that she rattled off her past in a monotone. She didn't miss out a single detail, yet, did not let those details affect her. She didn't even skip the parts where she attempted suicide— thrice.

'I thought that I could leave my son behind in the care of the doctors and nurses. That he would grow up in the hospital.'

2001-2003

Jamila *apa* ran an organisation, Shaheen Resource Centre, out of Buqshi Bazar in Old Hyderabad. She was also friends with the school principal where Sultana had briefly taught while she was completing school.

Jamila apa met her at the hospital. That was the turning point.

2017

'She was the first to tell me I was brave and strong and that I had to live for my child.'

2001-2005

Jamila apa got her a sewing machine. She spoke to Sultana's brother, who once again agreed to keep her. Sultana sewed and contributed to the income of the family. This time around, the neighbours weren't up in arms.

When her son turned three, getting him admitted into a good school started playing on her mind. There had to be more than the tailoring money. Once again, she met Jamila apa.

72

2017

'She took me in. There were trainings of all kinds, but most importantly, there was legal help for survivors of domestic violence.'

This was the little spark that she needed to get the fire going. She decided to pursue her case and filed a chargesheet.

2003 onwards

Not only did her father refuse to stand by her, he chided her brother for supporting her. Once again, the same remarks—'she is going to spoil your wife too'—was thrown at his face. Her sister-in-law stepped in and took Sultana in. She visited the Centre with her and liked the way Sultana was shaping up.

She promised to take Sultana's side, and to do all she could to make sure that her son was never separated from Sultana.

Visits to the police station were unnerving, to say the least. They said, 'I must have slept with another man. Why I didn't come immediately after the incident?'

One could sense a smirk in her tone. 'It was their mistake. Back then, they didn't take my statement properly because of which, he was let go within a few days of his arrest. Later, he ran away to Mumbai, and married another woman.'

Perhaps this was the time she made a resolve to punish her husband, fight her case till the very end, and fight for other women.

She filed attempt to murder, cheating and domestic violence cases against the husband. The sister-in-law paid for the lawyer. He was arrested. She demanded maintenance. He had to pay up.

2014

The trajectories of these two lives were so different that it is tough to imagine that there was a time when they were one.

The husband was in jail and his health had deteriorated. She saw him for the last time to identify him at the hospital. He died within seven days.

Sultana, on the other hand, had become a counselor in Shaheen. She was being recognised and felicitated for her work. She was traveling to the US and Bangladesh, talking about her work, and soaking up every bit of knowledge on tackling domestic violence. She made the trip to the US all by herself.

2017

Her son had turned 17. When they had gone to the court for hearings the first time, he was seven. He did get worried.

'Scared, actually.'

2010

He was about nine when he was kidnapped by the father. At this point, Sultana filed for custody and put him in a hostel.

When he was 10, she brought him with her to the Centre during one of the training sessions. This was his first brush with the gender discourse. What struck him the most was the session on roles of father and mother.

A week later, at the child custody hearing the judge asked him, 'What is your mother's name?'

'Sultana Begum.'

What settled the matter, however, was the answer to the next question.

'What is your father's name?'

'Sultana Begum.'

Glossary:

Dehleez: threshold

Doli: palanquin

Arthi: bier; The reference implies that once a girl is married and sent off, she should never leave her marital home under any circumstances. This mindset is one of the biggest propagators of domestic violence in India, and perhaps many countries.

Lost Voices

Brindarica Bose, Switzerland

For two years Monica had not taken any holidays. Her colleagues had already warned her that she would soon get burnout if she continued working this

77

way. Monica had also been a single parent and the primary caretaker for her nine-year-old daughter for the last three years.

As a research supervisor in Zurich Hospital, her hours were erratic. Even with Hans—her ex-husband helping whenever he could, life was way too hectic. This weekend was her birthday, so she had taken Friday off. After dropping her daughter for a play date at a friend's place in the afternoon, she went to a nearby cafeteria, determined to take some time off.

An English newspaper was lying on her table, and Monica pulled it towards her after ordering a Cafe Latte. It was almost 15 years since she lived in Zurich, yet her preferred language was always English and rarely German—a grudge Hans always had against her.

The front cover of the newspaper had featured a mural, which immediately attracted her attention. It was a colourful drawing of a woman swimming in mossy-green water, with her ankles chained to a baby, who was also trying to remain afloat. The woman was trying to reach an empty dinghy in the horizon.

The mural spoke to her at a different level. Being an art lover herself, Monica saw more, than the crude lines could depict. Her eyes lingered on the mural for few more seconds. She could identify herself with this woman painted on the wall of this Cox Bazar refugee camp in Bangladesh.

Who had drawn it? She wondered.

There was a report about a Rohingya refugee camp in Cox Bazar, and photo of a young woman artist—a survivor who had an amazing story to tell.

The caption read—'*Rohingya refugee artist, rediscovers her voice with art.*'

Monica turned to the next page.

In the middle of the page, there was another mural, featuring a woman standing in the middle of a forest. She was surrounded by dark brown branches trying to hold her back. This was another mural that the same artist had produced.

Both these photos had touched a chord. Monica felt connected to the artist in a strange way.

She started reading the article.

'*Days of heavy rainfall have pelted the Rohingya refugee camps in southern Bangladesh, destroying dwellings and sending thousands of people to live with extended families in communal shelters. In just 24 hours from Tuesday to Wednesday, more than 30 cm of rain fell on the camps in the Cox Bazar district, which houses more than a million refugees. Amidst this mess, the colourful walls created by some refugees who have taken to art as their last resort speaks of immense courage and resilience. Noori Begum, a 25-year-old amateur artist, who had lost her voice due to trauma, a resident of the refugee camp since 2018, drew these beautiful murals (two photos). An interview with Noori Begum follows, with our correspondent John Bruschi.*'

Noori's story was unique. She was a survivor, and she had learned how to be resilient using creativity as a tool.

Monica kept reading...

One morning, as Noori was returning from the factory close to the village Inn Dinn, where she worked as a textile worker, she received the news that the Burmese army had shot her father during a random shooting incident. He had been rushed to the hospital by neighbours. After a week, her father's left leg had to get amputated.

The army had already attacked their neighbouring village, and now they were closing on to theirs. Few families from their village were planning to flee, and Noori decided to leave with them, leaving her only home for the past 21 years. Nothing could be taken, except for a few clothes and the little savings that they had.

Noori's father had to be carried in a sling part of the way. Noori's uncle and a cousin, took turns to carry him. Thankfully her mother was fit enough to walk.

Noori was panic-stricken and couldn't believe what was happening around her. Every hour was fraught with terror and a sticky fear of getting caught any moment. What if the Burmese army came in the middle of the night? She couldn't sleep, even when they rested.

It took them three days to arrive at the river bank. From there, rescue teams would help them reach an international camp, as other fleeing refugees had claimed. But Noori was afraid. Something deep inside her had sealed off all sounds and words. She felt a pre-warning that the army would capture them mid-way.

Eventually, Noori and her family arrived at the border. And so did the Burmese army. Surrendering to the army was inevitable.

There was no way she could hide her father lying in a sling, and her hysteric mother not wanting to leave his side.

But due to a stroke of luck, within just a few hours of captivity, they got rescued by a team of Red Cross volunteers. A photojournalist had alerted the Red Cross on time. Doctors and paramedics rushed to take Noori's father and all rescued refugees to safety. Noori's family moved into a refugee camp at Rohingya Cox Bazar, Bangladesh since then.

All was going well, but instead of sighing in relief, Noori realised that she had lost her voice all of a sudden. She couldn't speak coherently at all!

To her despair and panic, even her scream sounded like a muted whisper. The doctor in the refugee camp said this was a post-traumatic reaction and that it would eventually heal.

But it stayed, and so did her nagging fear of getting caught by the Burmese army.

Her nightmares had captured her voice instead.

The camp was full of all sorts of men. Good as well as those with hungry, vacant eyes and no work. The monsoon and the torrential rains didn't help either. There was stark poverty and a depressive environment everywhere.

In the beginning of 2020, an international NGO came to the Rohingya refugee camp with a project to paint murals. Unable to talk, Noori had been drawing on small pieces of papers that she showed to a volunteer. The NGO's foreign volunteer seemed pleased with those drawings and gave her a brush and some colours, and prodded her to paint on a brick wall. What Noori produced astonished them both!

The transition, as well as the transformation, was not easy. But Noori kept at it, determined to take the first step. She tried to protest against her handicap. But still, her throat remained parched, bereft of speech.

But she kept painting, and helping others paint murals. The NGO had provided them with sufficient supply of paints and brushes. A year went by in this tug of war, between 'giving up hope' and 'waking up with courage' to endure and deal with another day.

The day the photographer from New York Times came, Noori showed him the walls which she had painted. Noori was an art-leader teaching others by then, in the refugee camp. Those photos went viral when the correspondent posted them in social media. After few months, another journalist arrived to cover Noori's story.

That is when the miracle happened.

82

With every brushstroke, an invisible rope across Noori's throat started loosening. The day finally arrived, when she could whisper her first few coherent words again; *'Ami benche achi,'* *(I am still alive, in Bengali).*

Noori's story had become the story of resilience and the therapeutic power of art was at the forefront.

.   ...

Monica folded back the newspaper and got ready to leave the cafeteria with renewed hope. Noori's story, her struggle, her resilience compelled her to reflect back on her own life. Her struggles seemed so insignificant in comparison to what Noori had undergone and survived. Monica felt gratitude towards her own life, and realised the possibilities that she had to transform not only her own life, but also to help others. Monica, jotted down the NGO's name, determined to reach out, and made a mental note, to buy a canvas and few paint brushes from the papeterie, her colour box had to be retrieved from the attic soon.

Epilogue:

This story is based on a report published in The New York Times in March, 2021, and the work of an NGO Artolution. Artolution is a New York-based arts education non-profit working in global crisis zones that include refugee camps in southern Bangladesh, where roughly 740,000 Rohingya fled in 2017. The organization's mission is to deploy the arts as a humanitarian tool.

The Tale of the Travelling Talisman

Anamika, Australia

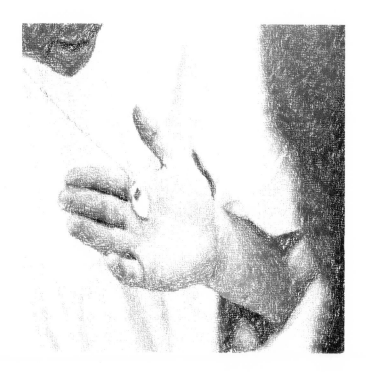

What would you do with a gift that has changed your life—keep it or give it away?

That is the dilemma I faced almost thirty years ago as a new mother.

85

A young banker making my way up the corporate ladder at the time—with all the right academic credentials from the right institutions—my life had no room for blind faith or superstition.

Growing up in Kolkata, often considered the intellectual heart of India, my Brahmin upbringing at home sat comfortably with the Christian world-views of the Irish nuns at my school. If pushed, I would have described myself as spiritual rather than religious, and I hadn't thought twice before marrying into a Catholic family. Yet one sunny day in late 1992, as I listened to an old friend pouring his heart out for his firstborn who lay ill in a Chennai hospital, my thoughts were turning to divine intervention, and an event, I can only describe as miraculous.

I still get goosebumps thinking about that conversation, recalling how my fingers had automatically reached for the little medallion around my neck as I heard his sad news, holding onto it for strength as I had done throughout my own difficult pregnancy. Could Mother Teresa's gift help my friend too? As always, it's reassuring presence had helped to soothe my anxiety. '*Deep breaths, clear your mind, and focus on the moment you felt Mother's calming presence that terrible evening,*' the voice in my head had said.

The evening in question, more than twelve months earlier in mid-August 1991, an uncontrollable rage had coursed through me as I vented my anger on my husband. Our cozy little marital nest had suddenly turned into a prison as I lay confined to my bed, unable to stop the bleeding that belied a positive pregnancy test. That very day my gynaecologist had delivered a stark message—we needed to prepare ourselves for a miscarriage if the haemorrhaging had not stopped in a day or so.

How unfair was it that I had to endure not just the nausea and heartburn of early pregnancy, but also the crushing guilt of threatening the life of our unborn child every time I moved, while my husband was free to lead a perfectly normal life. We had both worked so hard to get our professional lives on-track before we married—yet I was now unable to return to the job I loved, my colleagues were being handed my hard-won clients, and my boss was beginning to voice concerns about how long he could leave my position vacant, given the uncertainty about my health.

'*Why is this happening to me?*' I yelled.

My husband's usual stoic silence just served to fuel my frustration that evening—did he not understand - or worse, did he not care?

The walls of the little flat I had so lovingly made into a home just a few short months ago now seemed to be closing in on me, compounding a crushing sense of helplessness as my own body was now failing me.

With every movement, I risked losing the precious life that had taken a tenuous hold in my womb.

Suddenly, in the midst of my tears and rage, I felt an inexplicable sense of calm—as if a cool white light was caressing me, gently releasing the tension from every muscle as it travelled from my forehead down to my toes.

My husband, startled by the sudden silence, walked quickly back into the room—I could see he was probably wondering whether I had fainted. Yet I no longer wanted to yell at him, or to force him to feel my pain. Instead, I recall feeling oddly detached, as if I were observing myself lying on the bed, all traces of anger and recrimination wiped away. That night I rested peacefully after weeks of uneasy sleep.

The next morning, we were woken by my mother-in-law. Our weekly ritual of sharing a meal after attending church with my in-laws had been abruptly interrupted by my illness. '*I have a very special surprise for you*' my mother-in-law said, holding out her hand—and sitting there I saw an ordinary little medallion bearing Mother Mary's image, indistinguishable from thousands that are handed out daily at churches across India.

Even as I puzzled over what was so special about this small piece of metal, my mother-in-law threaded it onto my necklace, urging me to wear it at all times.

She went on to explain that the previous evening, after wrapping up choir practice with the nuns at Shishu Bhavan (Mother Teresa's orphanage where she regularly volunteered) she had felt compelled to offer a prayer for me in their chapel.

As she knelt at the altar, she was surprised to find Mother herself entering the chapel and sitting beside her. Hearing about my illness, Mother joined her in prayer, and then handed her the little medallion, saying '*Give this to your grandson.*'

I was dumb-struck as I heard this—could it be a coincidence that I had felt a calming peace traverse my body at the very same time that Mother Teresa had been praying for me?

I was not Catholic or even particularly religious, nor did I believe in miracles. Dare I hope that despite the grim fate the doctors were predicting, Mother's gift might help me bring a healthy child into this world?

I found myself reaching for the medallion, drawing strength from its comforting presence. And from that day onwards—much to my doctor's surprise - I stopped bleeding and went on to deliver a healthy baby in early 1992, despite a complicated pregnancy.

In a few short months I was back at work and promoted to a busy role, trying hard to balance mother-hood with a promising career.

A chance visit to Chennai for a training course later that year, gave me an opportunity to catch up with an old friend who had just become a father. As soon as I saw him though, I realised that all was not well—with tears in his eyes he explained that his son had arrived prematurely and was critically ill.

His wife was inconsolable, living in constant fear of losing her precious child.

Only a miracle could help them now, I heard him say.

My fingers reached for the little medallion around my neck, holding onto it for strength as I had done throughout my difficult pregnancy.

Mother Teresa's gift had brought my son safely into this world—could it help this little family too?

A million thoughts ran through my mind as my friend described his heartache, oblivious to my internal battle.

Dare I give her gift away? What if I needed it again? Would my friend, a practising Hindu, share my faith in Mother's medallion? Would he treat it with respect? What if he lost it?

By the time he paused for breath though, I had made up my mind. His need was greater than mine, and his little boy deserved the same chance as my own son.

I unclasped the medallion from my necklace and pressed into his hand. Startled, he asked what I was doing.

So, I shared my story with him, and asked him to offer Mother's gift to his wife. If she did not want to keep it, I made him promise he would mail it back to me, as I had to leave for home the next day.

I did not hear from him for a while, and was reluctant to follow up in case all was not well—but in a couple of weeks I received his call.

Although his parents had not warmed to the idea of adding Mary's image to the *puja-thaali* full of flowers they brought each day, blessed by the *pandit* in their

90

temple, his wife had insisted—so these objects from different faiths now lay side by side in the hospital room.

His wife often held onto the medallion, he said, as she recited the *Hanuman Chalisa* for their son.

Over the next little while, we kept in touch as the baby slowly but surely gained strength, and before too long, he rang with the joyous news that the doctors were finally ready to perform the life-saving surgery his little boy needed. Some six months after the fateful day on which I had met him in Chennai, I received a courier package from my grateful friend—the humble little medallion, now resplendently washed in 22-carat gold!

The very next year saw my family migrating from Kolkata to Melbourne, Australia where I continued to work for the same bank.

Of course, Mother's gift went with us, safely worn around my neck till the day I met a colleague at a conference in Canberra, whose autistic daughter had been diagnosed with a terminal illness. A proud leader in his local Aboriginal community, he was struggling to stay strong for his family as they tried to cope with the terrible news.

This time, Mother's medallion stayed with his family till the child passed away peacefully many months later. He mailed it back to me with a beautiful note, saying it had given them the strength to let her go.

By now others at the bank had heard the tale of the medallion, so I was not surprised when a member of my team, a self-proclaimed atheist whose wife was pregnant after many unsuccessful IVF attempts, asked to borrow it. He said he was embarrassed to admit it, but his wife had been pestering him to bring the medallion home, having heard my story at an informal team lunch.

This time, it came back to me with a framed photo of their beautiful twins—a pigeon pair of a healthy boy and girl – which is still on display in my home.

In the many years that have since passed, Mother's gift—I call it the 'travelling talisman'—it has traversed the globe many times, changing lives as it passes from one troubled family to another.

At times, a friend I have entrusted it to, has sought permission to pass it on to someone else in need, yet the little medallion has always found its way back home to me.

I still do not believe in blind faith or superstition, yet I know that this ordinary piece of metal has somehow brought comfort and solace to all those who have put their faith in it, irrespective of caste, creed or religion. If that is not miraculous, what is?

As I share this tale, my 'travelling talisman' is safe with a friend in India who is recovering from post-traumatic stress. His job, which exposes him to life-threatening situations on a daily basis, is difficult - yet he feels duty-bound to continue to serve his country. He says the medallion, which accompanies him everywhere, keeps him focused on everything that is positive in his life. When he apologises for having held onto it for so long, I say *When you are strong enough, you will find yourself giving it away to someone who needs it more than you.'*

Epilogue:

I am a very ordinary person who had an extraordinary experience many decades ago. I do not know whether you, dear reader, would view my medallion as a divine intervention or a miracle. All I know for sure is that Mother Teresa's gift helped me to face impossible odds with courage, and continues to bring me comfort, even though I no longer have it with me. My mother, on the other hand, often says that what is truly miraculous is that I have found the strength to give it away.

Glossary:

Puja-thaali: Metal tray with flowers / food items used in Hindu religious ceremonies.

Pandit: Hindu priest.

Hanuman Chalisa: A Hindu devotional hymn with 40 verses in praise of Lord Hanuman, the protector and granter of boons. Its repeated chanting is said to have the power to sweep away all ills, grant human wishes and provide protection from evil spirits.

Confidente

Ashwathy Menon, India

'Can I attend the meeting as well? I think I will be able to contribute to the strategic aspect of the project.'

There was a moment of silence at the breakfast table. Shanaya's father, Sujeet cleared his throat and mumbled with a half-hearted smile, 'I think you could brief Alok, and he could take it from there. It is a high-profile meet with only key managers involved. You could maybe join once the project kicks off.'

Shanaya smiled and nodded. She knew the response well enough. She just wanted to test the waters. No matter how good her suggestions or inputs would be, she knew her parents would avoid having her partake in client meetings related to their business.

'Come on, Alok! Hurry up. Surely you do not want to walk into that meeting late,' said Shanaya's mother Arunima animatedly, trying to steer away from the awkward moment. Alok gobbled up his remaining food and got up, patting Shanaya on the back gently, giving her an understanding nod, and rushed towards the exit door.

After watching her family leave, Shanaya dragged herself to her room and closed the door behind her. She sat down on the bed in despair. She wanted to scream, let her anguish flow through her tears, but none of it would happen. She just could not cry. Her tears had dried as she had grown up, trying to deal with her disability and coping with the reality.

It wasn't the disability that bothered her—it was the attitude of people towards it that crippled her. All she wanted was: equal treatment and not being reminded of being *special* or not being enough!

96

She walked towards the mirror and removed her jacket. She stared at those short *ugly* arms of hers that were deformed. Diagnosed with *skeletal limb abnormality* at birth, Shanaya was looked down upon as the unlucky one in all generations of their business family.

When the eldest, supposedly the heir of the family, is born with a congenital defect, it leads to a lot of dejection among the senior members of the family. As if that was not enough, she was always the talk of social gatherings, the centre of all conversations, how unlucky were the 'Sindal Group of Companies!' Shanaya wanted to scream at all of them, telling them it was not her fault and that they should mind their mess, but instead, she simply chose to avoid those-so-called social gatherings of the business group.

Reserved by nature, Shanaya had no close friends. Her social circle was that of the business group families, and none of them seemed interested in breaking the wall that she had built around herself. Alok was the only one who understood her a little bit but felt weighed down under the expectations laid upon him by the family. He seldom retorted to anything and tried hard to grasp the nuances of business, something he was not inclined towards naturally.

Shanaya had the business acumen but the family refused to acknowledge it. Shanaya remembered and empathised with the scion of Bharata Dynasty, Dhritarashtra, *and* felt his pain. The only difference here was that she felt no animosity towards Alok for he had been forced to take over the reins of the business.

Shanaya loved to learn, and it was this constant effort to upgrade her knowledge that kept her glued to the laptop, her constant, most trustworthy, and sole companion.

It was a Saturday afternoon and, while she was browsing through some websites, an advert about a TEDx talk popped up on the screen. It read *The Opportunity in Adversity*, the speaker being a wheel-chair-bound businesswoman named Ahaana Kamat. 'Wow!' exclaimed Shanaya. She knew she *had* to attend this event. Shanaya headed to the site immediately and booked a seat for herself. The event was scheduled a week from then, and time always seemed to crawl as you longingly waited for something. Restless, Shanaya counted days and minutes left for the event.

Finally, the D-day arrived, and Shanaya dressed in a formal outfit accompanied by a jacket. For the first time, she felt like dressing up. There was something about this day that made her feel different. Adorning herself with a pearl set and a branded watch, she walked with elan towards the car. If Shanaya were not to remove her jacket, one would not even notice the missing arms for a second.

The show was to begin in the next ten minutes. Shanaya settled herself in the front row. She did not want to miss anything due to distance, hence, booking a seat in the prime section. Two minutes into the introduction wheeled in Ahaana—a young, charming woman radiating confidence and belief. Shanaya did not notice anything beyond Ahaana's smile and charm.

The only true disability is a crushed spirit!

Look at you (she pointed at Shanaya's elegant sense of style). You have so much to be grateful for, and I could only assume you most certainly do not lack opportunities. There is so much that you can offer to yourself, as well as the world!'

Shanaya was at a loss for words. Realization dawned - it was *her* that she needed to take control of! *Take control of her thoughts instead of expecting others to change their thoughts about her.* It was, in that profound moment, she realized that it was *she* who had not come to terms with her physical condition.

Her condition was not that of a progressive degenerative ailment and she was independent as far as personal needs were concerned.

The negative bubble she had been trapped in needed to burst. She suddenly saw a flurry of positives that she had been blessed with!

'You are so right, Ahaana. I need to recalibrate my thought process.'

'Glad to hear that, Shanaya. Be in touch. I am sure we can work together to bring about a change,' said Ahaana, extending her visiting card.

'Thank you. This means so much, I will surely meet you soon!' said Shanaya, enthusiastically.

Shanaya, on her way back, remained thoughtful.

She needed to set many things right, beginning with herself. *Why did she have this desire to join the family business? Why was she seeking acceptance from others? What stopped her from starting on her own? She knew she had the knowledge and the determination to do it.* She muttered a small prayer in gratitude for all the blessings in her life, and she knew then that her life was going to change thereafter.

Five years later:

Shanaya was handed over a letter by the attorney representing Ahaana. She was perplexed and accepted the letter with apprehension and anxiety. It was not even a day since she attended Ahaana's funeral, and she was still not able to come to terms with the loss of her mentor and best friend. Shanaya had joined Dignitate five years back under the guidance and mentorship of her idol.

The company had been nominated for that year's 'Award for Business Excellence' and she felt a sense of vacuum without Ahaana by her side.

Shanaya opened the letter with shaky hands.

The letter informed her that she was being appointed as the new CEO of Dignitate, with a significant shareholding in the company.

She knew it was not because she was from a business family or that she had the acumen to run it. Ahaana knew that it would only be Shanaya who would run the organization with passion, compassion and serve the purpose that it was formed with.

102

Shanaya was in tears.

This angel not only turned her life around but left a piece of her soul with her.

After a month, at the award ceremony, while receiving the award, Shanaya dedicated the award to Ahaana and announced a new initiative named *Confidente* —an organization that will counsel and mentor those in the greatest need for confidence; in memory of what her soulmate had done for her all those years ago.

Amidst all the cheer & claps, she looked up, smiled, and whispered,
'I miss your physical presence Ahaana, but I know you will be by my side forever!'

Glossary:

Dignitate: Latin word for Dignity
Confidente: A Spanish word for Confidant

Just Another Day

Thangam Pillai, India

The sultry heat woke her up.

Asha wiped the sweat with her saree pallu.

A soft smile played upon her lips as she remembered. As if to reassure her, a miraculous soft breeze blew across her face. She hoped against hope that it was not dawn yet and turned towards the other side pulling her six-year-old Kiran's skirt.

However, a deliberate cough from her mother-in-law, Ammaji, reminded her that this too was like any other day. She signed and sat upright on the tattered mat to mutter a few words invoking lord Ganesh's guidance and protection.

She got up and washed her face with the precious mug of water that she saved from last night and brushed her teeth in the same drain which doubled up as her private corner, a luxurious extension to her kitchen amongst the overcrowded "*chawl*" in Bombay.

Feeling refreshed she looked at the broken piece of mirror that she had hung at the corner. Asha looked no different today. She peered carefully at her luscious hair, face smooth as ever without a hint of a wrinkle. She smiled.

'Agahh..' the cockerel's sound started getting louder. She rushed out with the buckets and pots, 'I have set the water to boil for tea, Ammaji. Just keep an eye on it while I fetch the water.'

The old lady hobbled out of her bed when she heard the water boiling.

'What is the point of having a daughter-in-law? All my life, I had to serve my mother-in-law. At least, at

106

the fag end of my life I deserve some rest. But Nah! Not in my destiny!!'

'Even with a son, daughter-in-law and a granddaughter, I have to burn in the kitchen to get an ounce of warm drink!' So, mumbling the octogenarian reduced the flame to a minimum when the water started boiling rather than expediting the tea-making process by adding some tea dust to it.

'Ammaji, why did you reduce the flame? You could have put the *chai patti* no?' continued the grumbling old lady, mimicking Asha uncannily.

Today, surprisingly, Asha merely smiled and proceeded to make tea for everyone. Spinning around the house for about three hours, Asha made sure everyone had their bellies and tiffin boxes filled. Even Ammaji's lunch was kept on the makeshift table near the TV. Washed clothes laid out to dry on the lining running through the house, so that they were dry by the time folks were back home.

Asha hurried to change into her high-necked salwar kameez, stitched loosely with coarse material. Today, she wore her only silk pants. They were soft on her skin but would stick to her body in the sweltering Mumbai humidity. She held her coarse *salwar* as if mentally answering the catcalls which she knew she would face, regardless of what she wore. Just as she thought she was done, she stopped to look at herself in the small mirror perched near the shelf and smiled at herself.

She rummaged through her suitcase and picked out her precious lipstick carefully wrapped inside the saree. She did not dare to apply it amply, but merely a wisp of it on her finger.

Rubbing away the pesky little droplets of sweat on her face, which seemed to stubbornly appear she stealthily applied this luxury on her lips.

Asha looked over to make sure Ammaji was engrossed in the TV and went to the "*father* of her children," in the hope to catch his eye.

He was busy searching for a bag to buy the vegetables. 'I will get the vegetables and fruits!'

The plush supermarket near his office used to clear the stale vegetables for fresh ones and the older ones were sold at half the cost which he used to buy religiously. He used to walk an extra half a Kilometre to make sure he can at least indulge his kids in high-class fruits.

'Where is the bag?' he looked around irritably when Asha came and caught his eye. Something was different in her. Was it a twinkle that he just saw in her eyes?

'Aayi I told you to get me a pencil! You forgot again?' cried her daughter.

'She didn't get it because I told her not to!' He chimed in defending her quickly.

'But why Papa?' continued the adorable little one, redirecting her gaze but this time with a pout.

'Well Raghu mama had only black pencils. My Gudiya rani likes coloured pencils, right?'

Today he has promised to get coloured ones. Today aayi will get coloured ones for you! Right aayi?' Asha nodded smilingly and patted her daughter asking her to get dressed. She then rolled her eyes and accosted the father of her child, 'Coloured pencils cost one Rs more! You spoil her.'

She was still peeved at the unnecessary indulgence when she walked her daughter to the school-rickshaw.

As he left for his work, the father wondered what the fleeting twinkle in her eyes was about. Just as he was pondering, his bus came and he hurried to get into the crowd, all the thoughts and twinkle left behind.

Walking to her work was a nightmare with the leering men, dirty and dusty roads, jostling hawkers, platforms turned into a crowded dirty makeshift market —that was till she discovered the beautiful world of her own!

The twinkle in her eyes returned as she fixed her earplugs into her ears, cancelling out all the unwarranted attention and the grossness of "real" life.

With her specs also tucked away she was oblivious to the morose, frustrated, overwhelming crowd in the street. This was her favourite world and her me-time. She was not only enjoying herself but doing so without feeling guilty.

As a woman brought up conventionally there are very few joys that she could enjoy without feeling guilty.

She reached the stationery shop, with a frown on her brow as the neighbouring sweet vendor leered at her, almost blocking her way while clutching a *jalebi* in his dirty hands.

He called her name loudly so that she couldn't feign indifference. The pervert stood right in front of her and thrust the sweet towards her, almost touching her breasts as he ogled her shamelessly.

She saw across to find that her boss had not reached the shop. She shoved him away with her umbrella and entered the shop and pulled down the wooden half door across and said gruffly, 'I don't eat sweets.'

The owner walked in just then muttering, 'Today's girls! No culture, no manners and absolutely no etiquette!'

Asha merely went about doing her work. She doubled up: taking charge of production (taking photo-copies and typing out letters and scanning them and helping people email) and providing customer support (handling the customers, negotiating the prices). She was on her feet the full day except for the half an hour when the shop had closed for lunch and the brief respite that she had between customers.

110

By evening her secret bubble of happiness had vanished as she walked back deadened inside out.

Even her earplugs could merely cancel out additional jeers and leers but not pull out an ounce of positive strength.

She reached home to find the house empty. So relieved did she feel that the hint of the smile fluttered on her lips. She quickly threw her bag and rummaged through her shelf and pulled out a towel thinking of taking a long bath.

One look at the water pots and she realized that most of the water has already been consumed by the family leaving her just enough for her kitchen which reminded her of the ominous tasks of cooking and folding the clothes looming ahead of her.

Oh! how she longed for a bath! She even dabbled with the idea of buying a can of water which would cost at least fifty Rupees. Just then the cable guy called asking if he could come down to collect his seventy-five rupees which were already overdue.

Poor ammaji, cable tv was her only solace in the city since she came here. Asha decided to forgo the bath and just took a mug of water to wash her face and legs in the alley attached to her kitchen.

Asha sat down in her "corner" looking at the mirror, feeling very broken and was filled with pity for the tired face staring at her from the mirror. Suddenly unbridled tears started flowing as she mumbled. 'God, don't I deserve a single bath?' Just then Ammaji hobbled

111

in calling out, 'Asha oh Asha, come here! See the door is left wide open! I don't know when this girl will learn!'

Asha wiped away her tears and went to the door when she saw ammaji carrying a tiffin box. 'I asked our neighbours to cook dinner for us today!' she smiled toothlessly and continued, 'And see I have saved one bucket of water for you to take a bath. Now don't just stand there gaping. Take a bath before your husband and kids come. They have gone to buy a cake. It is your *Janam divas na?*'

Asha stood aghast and didn't notice that she was smiling.

'What do they say nowadays?? Happy b-day!!' pronounced the octogenarian grittily

'Now go keep the food in the kitchen!'

The next morning still felt glorious.

Asha decided to take a day off as it was Saturday. She called her boss but he did not pick up so she sent a message and busied herself with the day-to-day chores. She decided she would cook something special. The celebratory mood struck around in the house and everyone was smiling more than usual.

She was happily cooking when her phone rang. Somehow, she knew that it was bad news. Her boss fired her.

With her mind swirling under the blow, she wordlessly served lunch and lay down for a nap. Her daughter snuggled next to her and said, 'Aye I know you can't go to work tomorrow. I am so happy. You will eat with me every day!' cried excitedly.

'Didi' Devi, her neighbour, walked in announcing, 'Please print this out for me. I need it for Monday.' She thrust her pen drive into Asha's hands.

Asha could not hold it any longer.

She burst into tears. 'I lost my job.'

After a long chat Devi's words struck in Asha's mind.
'Start a shop of your own!'

At night the whole household was drowned in an air of melancholy but Asha was busy on the phone talking and making notes. She finally got up and announced, 'I need fifty thousand to buy a printer, computer and scanner. I am going to start a shop here.'

Her husband looked at her helplessly, conveying everything in those few silent moments. Asha sat down totally broke and started crying inconsolably.

Ammaji got up wordlessly and went to her and thrust a wad of dirty notes wrapped in a piece of old cloth. Asha counted it and found around sixty thousand in it.
Nine months later:

'There is no place in this house, and this maharani has bought "capier" machine. She will throw

113

all of us out and fill the house with computers!' grumbled Ammaji.

Asha smiled as she applied her favourite colour of lipstick. She had few of them now. Asha looked at the mirror to find a "Ma'am" who not only managed a photocopying shop but also trained the children in computer and internet. She wore a tad more fashionable dresses, and most importantly had lunch with her children every day!

The Miracle Child

Nandini Sircar, UAE

On waking up, a disappointed Miremba
Sebugwaawo leaned forward to pick up the newspaper
that was lying on the parapet outside her house.

She read the morning paper in complete disbelief. She threw the newspaper aside and quickly reached out for her phone.

Miremba's head was pounding and her heart was thumping. Her eyes were not only filled with fear but also with gratitude.

The battery of her mobile had drained and the phone was dead. She was frantically looking for the charger now. As soon as she managed to switch on her phone, the mobile beeped incessantly with umpteen unread messages.

Her ailing mother back home had tried her phone innumerable times the previous night. Miremba was due to leave for Kampala (Uganda) to be with her mother who was battling cancer.

Things were coming to Miremba in a flash back now. She was to leave office for her annual leave the previous evening and had tried winding the day early, when a breaking news alert at the last moment compelled her to stay longer than she had imagined. Her seniority and expertise as a journalist warranted her presence at work.

Reluctantly opening her laptop bag again, while making a few hurried calls to her contacts, Miremba had impatiently looked at her watch every few minutes, while mentally calculating the time it would take to reach the Dubai International Airport from her *NationTimes* office in Al Quoz, Dubai.

Her delay at work had saved her life. She could not board the ill-fated flight to Entebbe.

But her cousin who was supposed to travel with her the previous evening had boarded the flight that crash landed just a few kilometers ahead of the Entebbe International Airport.

Trying to reach her cousin's phone proved to be futile now. She then tried to get in touch with an airport officer whom she had known for years professionally.

A voice at the other end said, 'Hello, Miremba.'

'Hello Mahwash,' said an anxious Miremba.

'I was trying to find out about my cousin who was on board the flight that crashed last night. His name is Irumba Sebugwaawo. How can I get his details, please guide me. Are there any survivors?' Miremba was choking up.

'Yes, there are. After two unsuccessful landing attempts due to bad weather, the plane tried to touch down on the runway but couldn't. The aircraft did not stabilize and instead it spun downwards - perhaps due to some mechanical failure.'

'The locals heard a loud 'crackling' noise before it broke into separate pieces. But there are crash survivors who were seated at the rear half of the plane. Let's hope your cousin got lucky... fingers crossed. I'll find out. How old is he?' added Mahwash.

'31.' Miremba was quick to respond.

When she hung up, Miremba felt dizzy as she sat down on the couch. Conversations that she had with her cousin the previous evening, as he was preparing to head to the airport were running in her head now.

How excited Irumba had been to go back home for his wife's delivery who was due anytime now with their first child.

The two had fallen in love at a common friend's party and were quick to get married. The couple had been married a little over a year.

Miremba had assisted Irumba over every possible weekend, as the latter visited several malls in Dubai, going on a shopping spree, preparing to welcome his little one.

They had gone around visiting the well-known Dubai Mall, The Mall of the Emirates, Ibn Battuta Mall and the smaller neighbourhood shopping plazas.

Every other weekend was spent in children's stores last month.

Irumba had paid special attention to every detail, purchasing baby clothes, shoes, comb and even diapers and pacifiers, saying he couldn't find in Kampala what he found here. They knew they were welcoming a baby boy.

As Miremba was lost in thought the phone rang again. This time it was her mother.

'Maama,' said Miremba. 'I am trying to track Irumba. I've spoken to a friend in the aviation sector here. I'll let you know about him soon.'

'No Abbo, you don't have to,' said her mother. 'He is in the hospital in Entebbe. He has had multiple fractures and the doctors say he needs to undergo multiple complex surgeries.'

'Oh! Thank God! He is alive,' exclaimed Miremba.'Do let me know his condition, keep updating me…please,' she urged her mother.

'Yes, sure,' said her Mamma.

Miremba could hear the loud beep after her mother hung up.

Meanwhile, Miremba came back to her laptop, restlessly reading crash updates as she swiftly moved from page to page on different websites.

Some videos depicted horrific scenes of the accident as locals and medics rushed to save lives.

On a Ugandan website, Civil Aviation Authority spokesman Adroa Igundura in a video said that there were six crew and 184 passengers on board the aircraft when it crashed. 'The rescue is on right now,' he said.

New details kept emerging about the deadly plane crash with angry and worried relatives screaming in the video footage. Even foreign television channels were airing the unfortunate incident with running news tickers asking, 'What caused the accident?'

90 people were killed when the plane, during an emergency landing, came down near the Lido beach, breaking the aircraft into three, leaving debris scattered across several kilometres.

Preliminary news reports even suggested there was a small explosion after the initial crash with no possible survivors in that part of the plane.

'When it crashed, man, that's all you heard first, a loud thud. I ran towards the site, as I could faintly see a few people trying to jump out of the plane. I think I even saw a man with a child,' a fisherman told television reporters.

'The identities of the staff members whose lives were lost in this tragic accident are being released gradually to allow time to notify their loved ones,' Vistafly airlines said in a statement early Sunday. 'The cause of the crash is unknown at this time; the incident is under investigation,' the television anchor somberly read over red and white graphics that were running on the screen.

Miramba's eyes drifted from the television and she went back to her own childhood memories with

Irumba. The current turn of events seemed almost unreal to her.

As first cousins they lived in the same house in the Wakiso district, about 40 km from Kampala. She remembered the time when she was only seven. The two had been playing gleefully when Miramba suddenly slipped and fell from the parapet, bruising her knees. A very caring Irumba had rushed inside to get ice from the house. He hurriedly walked back with it, gently massaging the ice on her wound, to ease the pain.

Then her thoughts wandered to Masiko, Irumba's wife, and how she may have reacted to the news of the terrible incident.

Just then, Miramba's thoughts were abruptly disrupted by a sudden phone call.

It was her mother on the other side. 'Abbo, Masiko is in the labour room. When she heard the news of Irumba's accident, she started developing excruciating pain in her abdomen.'

'Even her water broke.'

'She has been admitted in the same hospital where Irumba is undergoing several emergency surgeries. He is in a critical condition. The impact of the crash has lacerated his brain and it's been swelling to a point that may be beyond repair. He may not make it, they are saying. Uhhh!…and Masiko is in the maternity ward,' added mamma.

121

Miramba's eyes swelled up with tears.

Irumba had not only been her closest cousin growing up together back home but it was Irumba who had urged her to come to the UAE and work, after her break up five years ago—a phase when she felt sad, angry and let down. Her cousin had been her emotional anchor motivating her to get over it quickly.

Her phone rang, it was Mamma again.

She was crying inconsolably.

'Doctors have written him off completely,' cried Abbo. But Masiko has delivered a baby girl. 'They say she is beautiful. The mother and child are stable,' she added. Miremba was at a loss for words.

The feeling of grief was overriding any iota of happiness at the moment.

She was choking as she hung up.

All she could think of was, '*Weeraba Irumba*' (Farewell Irumba). The weight of the day felt heavy on her. It seemed as if she was stuck in a hole with muddy walls. The harder she fought to climb out of it, the further entrenched she got.

A restless Miremba surfed several news websites while trying to book the earliest tickets back home to see her cousin one final time.

She could hear the phone ringing again. Was this the sounding of an ill omen?... she pondered.

'Abbo,' her mother had called again. Her heart skipped a beat.

'The unthinkable has happened. Masiko had entered Irumba's ICU with the baby. When the baby cried, Irumba's body shook, he flailed his arms and then...he slowly opened his eyes.'

'Irumba has started responding. Doctors stated it was nothing short of a miracle, Abbo,' said Mamma excitedly.

'I think the baby has brought good luck, Mamma,' Miremba smiled and thanked God silently as she hung up.

Ndi, Umunyarwandan

Raka Mitra, The Netherlands

Umwezi picked up the dusty broom and walked out slowly. She put one hand on her protruding belly and giggled at the responding "high five" from within.

A few more weeks now and he'd be out.

Her husband had tried to stop her from heading out today. 'Umu, it's not required for you!'

125

'Umuganda is for able bodied people! Sweeping the streets in this condition may impact the baby!'

Before she could protest, Mama spoke up, 'Let her go Emmanuel,' the older woman reached out to put her hand on Umuwezi's head, 'She needs to be with her mother today.' Emmanuel resigned, 'Okay, we can go together then today.'

Umunsi w'umuganda is a day of cleansing.

It is a day when every Rwandan between the ages of 18-65 takes to the streets to clean. For three hours, on the last Saturday of every month, the Nation comes together to clean.

In the first years of *Umuganda*, Umuwezi remembered the stockpiles of empty shell casings she used to find, a reminder of the darkness. Together they had cleaned the streets and now they beautified, pruning leaves and planting little flowering shrubs. 'The cleanest country in the world!' Kagame, their President had proclaimed, and indeed it was so.

She took Emmanuel's hand and they walked up to the hill at the end of their street.

It was a quiet spot, a dusty little clearing, with a neat green bench overlooking the fertile hills that embraced her country.

Young teens often came here in the evenings, to watch the sun set over the distant hills, so Umuwezi had found enough to clean up, a stray candy wrapper blown away in the breeze or a glass bottle left behind in haste.

Umuwezi however, loved this spot for different reasons. She loved it because if you looked to the hills from the bench, it faced her mother's village. The one from where they had run in those dark days, taking cover in the black night.

She could feel her mother's presence at this hill.

She felt the strong arms of her husband steady her from behind. She let herself fall back into his chest as his hands came around and cradled their unborn.

'She's here with us, always. They all are.' She put her own hand on his, and felt the dampness on his cheek nestled in hers. She didn't know if they were her own tears, or his. It didn't matter, for the lives they'd lived were one.

'Our baby will be the first in our family to have no connection to 1994,' he declared sombrely. She smiled at his naivety.

'Every child born to Rwanda has a connection to 1994.'

'Ey, but she will be a child of the future of Rwanda!'

'She?' she enquired amusedly. 'Yes, I feel it, Umuwezi, she will be like our mothers.'

Umuwezi could feel the corners of his lips stretch against her temple into a wide grin. Umuwezi loved that goofy smile, it had brought peace to her in times when her heart was in most despair. They both stood lost in their embrace, their thoughts carrying them over the lush green hills.

Umuwezi was just 6 when they had to run from their homes. Her family and her Aunt's family spent days taking cover in the thick forest. In the end it was just her and her Aunt left when they finally reached the United Nations camp.

The fallen bodies of their loved ones; parents, children, siblings and cousins had shielded Umuwezi and her Aunt. They had used death as a means to stay alive.

At some point, she had started calling her mother's sister 'Mama.' They clung to each other at night, each helping the other through their triggers and healing a little by little with each passing day.

Emmanuel had a similar story and with the help of some caring strangers the young boy had miraculously survived. The family that had helped him had since taken refuge in the United States.

'You should apply,' the 'Uncle' had advised him, 'You will get the visa too, you are orphaned!'

'Ndi, Umunyarwandan' he had simply said, *I am Rwandan.* His whole family lay in this land, their last breaths dispersed in the air around him and their blood coloured the red of the Rwandan soil.

The thought of leaving never entered his heart.

128

He stayed and worked hard to become a Nurse.

There was not a moment in which he regretted that decision, not even when he got emails and pictures of the good life in America that the Uncle and family had made for themselves.

That is also how he found Umuwezi, their lives had crossed in the hospital and he'd felt like he'd found family. The silent old woman with Umuwezi was always so gentle yet a bit skittish.

The day they met, the older woman had been brought to hospital by her beautiful young daughter. Some deep injury as a result of past trauma in the older woman's hip had been making it difficult for her to walk.

For the first few years, he didn't know that they weren't mother and daughter. He'd once inadvertently let his jealousy creep out, 'At least you have your Mama!' In any case, at least she had her Aunt.

He missed the smell of his own mother. The smell of red earth and the smoky smell of roasting *matoke* mingled with the sweet pungency of her days' work.

Some warm summer evenings when Aunty Mama, as he now called her, roasted *matoke* on the grill in their small garden, he would put his head in her lap and try to find that lost smell. Some days he almost did. She would quietly stroke his head as he cried into her skirt. Mama had lost too much herself, but in these two, Umuwezi and Emmanuel, she had found the four she lost. Keza, Kirezi, Nkunzi and her youngest, and only

129

son, Akimana. Umuwezi would often find Mama sitting on the bench on their hill, looking to the horizon, to the home they once had nestled in the fertile hills.

Mama made sure Umuwezi never forgot.

'Rwanda must look to the future, but she must never forget what happened!' she often said, when speaking of the genocide.

They had no pictures, but they shared stories often. Umuwezi couldn't remember her mother's face, so she would sometimes stare at her Aunt and search for similarities with her own mother. The eyes, the nose bridge and certain mannerisms sometimes helped her remember, her Aunt was mother's younger sister after all. The pain remained, but they learned to use memory as a healing balm on their yearning hearts.

Jolted back to the present by a giggle, Umuwezi pushed back against her husband in a moment of embarrassment, her friends were teasing them from the street below.

'Let her have this baby before you start planning for the second one Emmanuel!'

He turned to face them and that grin grew even wider. 'Ey, I am keeping her safe from you lot!' Umuwezi playfully swatted him away with her broom and just as she started to sweep under the bench, she felt a sharp cramp from deep inside her.

The moments that followed remained a blur to her, but her giggling girlfriends had swung to action under the guidance of her nurse husband.

He held her and comforted her as she gave in to the cues of her body. Mama had been summoned and also sat quietly guiding the young woman through a process as old as time.

They had tried to carry her home, but the contractions were too intense and they had all laughed at the sight of the 'hospital bag' laying on the dusty ground. An ambulance had been summoned, however 'life' had no time for plans.

As that life entered the mortal realms a stillness fell upon the intimate group gathered on that dusty hill. A moment of absolute wonder at the miracle of birth. In the next instant, a tiny wail broke the silence announcing her presence! 'It's a girl!' Mama beamed! Umuwezi and Emmanuel looked at each other and smiled at Mama.

"Kwazena," Umuwezi whispered, looking to the distant hills, willing the wind to carry the name to their families. "Hope" was a perfect name for the future of Rwanda. "Kwazena" they all repeated letting the name roll off their tongues and land as a blessing on the new-born, who was now nestled into her mother's breast, hungrily working on the semantics of suckling.

The sound of an ambulance siren spurred them to action. Umuwezi was left alone for a brief moment, while everyone gathered things and busied themselves with getting everything in order for a swift transfer.

131

Umuwezi looked around her, she looked at the small stain of dark red blood on the red dirt.

She had seen red blood on dirt before, but this time was so different. The same sight, all those years ago had filled her with a deadly fear, yet today it was the very symbol of life.

She breathed in, half expecting to smell death, but instead her lungs filled with the crisp Rwandan air with light notes of eucalyptus and a flower whose name she couldn't remember, but one whose fragrance often came to her on this very hill when she thought of her parents, sister and brothers.

For the first time, Umuwezi didn't feel any guilt for having lived, she looked down at the tiny fingers clutching her own and realised her destiny and that filled her with hope.

Epilogue:

I dedicate this to the survivors. I have spent countless hours reading your memoirs and whilst the horror makes you question the integrity of humanity, your stories of survival and resilience bring hope for humanity. To all those who perished, we, the world, failed you. We can only vow to never forget.

Glossary:

Umuwezi: Moon
Ndi, Umunyarwandan: 'I am Rwandan'
Umuganda: coming together for a common purpose
Umunzi w'umuganda: Day of community service
Matoke: green banana

The Little Girl from Barisal

Bidisha Chakraborti, US

Koloshgram, Barisal:

As the sky turned a vivid orange with the setting sun, signaling the passing of a very hot and humid late summer afternoon, Mr. Sengupta finished tying up the leather-bound accounts book with a sense of urgency.

135

A cashier with the Bengal Nawabs, his days were rarely dull, but today was different. There was a sense of nervous anticipation in his pace as he walked towards his home. As he took the last turn into the narrow lane, a small gathering of his neighbours huddled up at the entrance to his *uthon* lit up his tired, sweaty face with a smile.

It was time! He, his wife and their two young daughters were about to welcome the newest member to their family.

A few hours later, when the moon was high up in the sky, and a gentle monsoon breeze had cut through the balmy air, Monu Rani Sengupta entered the world, bawling at the top of her lungs. It was the middle of July in 1902.

Monu Rani was the third of five siblings. Her family of seven lived a humble but happy life in the small village of Koloshgram in Barisal district, pre-partition Bengal.

As a young girl, Monu was the life of her family. She was ever eager to learn what her father wrote in those books that he occasionally brought home from work.

Her ambitions were pure and the societal restraints on a girl child of that era were unknown to her at the time.

Every evening, she would hover near the edge of the *uthon* as her father washed his feet after returning home. '*Ore maa, ektu boshe ni!*' ('*My dear child, let me sit for a bit!*'), her father would often quip, amused at his young

136

daughter's enthusiasm to learn about numbers. It was this endless inquisitiveness that convinced her father to send her to the local primary school.

A girl going to school to study was not common for the rural towns of those days, and it often invited backlashes from the local community.

Monu Rani going to school raised eyebrows among her uncles and cousin brothers, who thought it was a waste of her time to sit and recite *bornomala* while she could be spending that time learning household chores. Thanks to her *baba*, Monu was guarded from many of these pressures.

Little did she know that her child-like innocence would be short-lived.

It was a crisp early afternoon in the autumn of 1910, a time when feathery, white *kaash phool* was blossoming in the wild fields behind Monu Rani's school.

The eight-year-old had just finished reciting *'Bristi Pare Tapur-Tupur'* by Rabindranath Tagore, along with her classmates. As she casually looked out of the window, she noticed Bhola *kaku*, her father's friend from work, walking across the fields towards her school. Something wasn't right.

'Why is he coming here?', Monu Rani thought.

Ten minutes later, as she was walking back home with *kaku*, she couldn't help but think how strange it was for her *master-moshai* to let her leave in the middle of a class.

As she entered her home's courtyard, she was surprised, and a tad bit anxious to see the space packed with people with sombre faces.

Something about the gathering unnerved her, and she quickly crossed over to her parents' room.

Her father was lying peacefully on a crisp white cloth on the floor, decorated with a thin garland. If it was not for her inconsolable mother being comforted by the ladies gathered in the room, and her siblings bundled up in a corner, it would have seemed that her father was taking a peaceful nap.

But life had just taken a cruel twist for the little girl. Monu Rani's father had passed away from a cardiac arrest, leaving her vulnerable in a world that had no place for a little girl's rising ambitions.

The days and months following the sudden demise of her father jolted the eight-year-old girl out of the innocence of childhood.

It brought along an increasing pile of debt for her family, with the loss of its sole earning member.

The little savings which her mother had reserved were depleting. To help her mother run the household, her uncles and cousin brothers stepped in as father figures.

The choice of education Monu Rani had when her father was alive and the dreams she had of becoming a teacher one day were slowly snatched away. She held on dearly to each remaining day of her time at school.

However, there was a disconcertingly increased frequency with which she was urgently ushered back from class to meet prospective grooms.

She was annoyed and upset but there wasn't much she could do. It wasn't long, after she turned 11, that her eldest uncle hurriedly came home one early evening with an elated look on his face and said, '*Monu shona, they like you!*'

She was going to be a bride, a child-bride like many of her friends in Koloshgram. She hadn't even seen the man she was marrying but this is what was expected of her.

The wedding was a small affair.

It was arranged by her uncles—to whom, Monu Rani's *maa* would often remind her to be grateful.

Against the background of *uludhoni* and *shonkho*, a sobbing, 12-year-old child bride, left her home, to start a new life with a man she had met just an hour ago. Soon the little girl started getting engrossed with household chores.

With each passing day, month and year, Monu Rani's curiosity dimmed, and memories from her school started to fade. All her aspirations of becoming a teacher seemed like a distant memory. She had accepted the fact that her life's path had changed, and the only future that mattered, was one with her husband.

She tried to be happy.

139

But as years went by, she realised that something was amiss.

There was something not quite right with her husband.

He wouldn't talk to her, and often had inexplicable fits.

At 17, Monu was no longer as naïve as she was, when she had just been married. She knew she couldn't ask questions, but she was angry that no one had told her about the challenges her husband had, in leading a regular life.

Someone must have known!

Her fears were soon confirmed.

One day, after another one of her husband's fits, Monu Rani had stepped out to calm her mind, when she overheard two of her neighbours, 'I feel sad for the poor girl... I didn't think the marriage would happen after what her family saw when they came to finalise the alliance!'

She couldn't believe what she had just heard. *Had she really been duped into marrying someone who, her family knew, was mentally unstable?*

Without thinking twice, she started walking towards her home.

No, it wasn't her home anymore, she corrected herself quickly mid-thought, her mother's home. She was oblivious of the mud from the unpaved road splattering her clean clothes, as she walked through the five-kilometre stretch.

She had questions that day.

Her fear of voicing her opinion had magically disappeared. It took only five minutes of talking with her mother, who just stared sadly at her most of the time, and with her uncles, to realise that her family had hid the condition of her husband from her.

Moreover, her uncles seemed incredulous that she had dared to even question the circumstances. As the incidents of the day unravelled in front of Monu, she felt betrayed and lonely, something extraordinary happened to her.

She was done crying and asking for the things which she considered was a basic right. It was almost as if a light lit within her that she realised she didn't want to live like this.

She went back, packed her small bundle of clothes, along with the only two books she possessed. She had little money, that she had saved, by helping other girls in the village tow water.

On a cold winter's day in 1920, Monu Rani left the house of her husband, never looking back once. She had no idea how her life would turn out, now that she was all by herself, but she was determined to change her fate.

With the help of her *master-moshai*, who was delighted to get one of his favourite students back, Monu went back to school to complete her education.

With no place to call home, she started living in an abandoned classroom, while trying to earn some money for food by doing any chores that paid.

It was probably one of the most challenging times for her. A married woman, who had left her marital home, was not taken kindly in those days.

With all social ties severed and nowhere to go, she soon started leaning on education. It gave her a sense of independence; she was soon helping her teacher take classes, and that also made her more money. However, despite her newfound independence, Monu kept getting pulled back into her troubled past.

As long as she stayed in Koloshgram, people there did not let her forget the 'sinful' act of leaving one's husband.

She had to leave town, if she wanted to have a fresh start. She used some of her savings to go to the Barisal district centre, and enrol in a teacher's training certificate program.

Used to receiving unapproving looks by then, she focused on getting through her training program for the next year.

Finally, in May 1925, a much more resilient Monu Rani, armed with her bag of books, and a brand-new teacher's training certificate, boarded the train for the longest journey of her life thus far. She felt eerily like when she had left her husband—determined to move forward, and never to look back. The difference this time, Monu thought to herself, as the train started the 14-hour journey north to Dinajpur, was the purpose that was firm on her mind. She had seen how literacy and education could help, and she was determined to dedicate her life to the quest of empowering young minds.

Dinajpur, Bangladesh:

Monu Rani was firm on her decision to commit her life to providing primary education to children, which could empower them to make their own choices. She established a primary school soon after landing in the town of Dinajpur, in present-day, northern Bangladesh.

Many years later, she would fondly remember the gratification and sense of pride she had felt, when the first batch of students had stepped in through the doors of her school. A couple of years later—sometime in mid-1927 - during one of her supply trips to the town centre, she came across a couple who were living next to the bookstore, in a makeshift shelter made of old sandbags.

As she approached them, she realised how severely malnourished the two of them looked.

Just as she was about to ask if they would like to eat something, she noticed that the woman was holding a half-asleep infant in her arms.

143

For a minute, Monu was instantly taken back to the days when she was trying to make ends meet to feed herself after she had left her husband.

Something overcame her, and she was surprised at the words that came out when she started to speak, 'I would be very happy to take care of your baby if you will allow me.'

The couple were relieved to have this burden taken off them. Monu Rani became a mother to baby Jiten Das, thus ending her solitary life.

As the years passed, and the baby grew into a toddler, and then into a young child, Monu Rani poured her heart into raising the child as her own. At a time when the concept of an adopted child was nearly unheard of, let alone one raised by a single mother, Monu Rani gave a new meaning to motherhood.

She did not need a piece of paper to decide what she felt for Jiten. Nevertheless, she did not ever want to keep him away from his biological parents. The parents were grateful in turn, and Monu Rani got a family who loved her; an adopted family, who she was not related to by any conventional means, but who chose to make her their own.

After years of struggle, Monu Rani finally had stability in her life, and a purpose that she was passionate about. She became known among the Dinajpur community as the headmistress who took in children and provided them with a foundation to build their lives on.

She had finally gotten her fresh start.

The rest of her life would probably have been uneventful if not for the partition of 1947.

Overnight, like many Hindu Bengalis, Monu's life was uprooted, as she joined thousands of others who were forced to leave everything behind and move across the border into refugee camps.

That night of August 14, 1947, Monu Rani had not just lost her home, but had to part ways with her adopted son who decided to stay back, not wanting to leave his biological parents.

Kolkata, India:

Monu Rani's life had never been easy, and over the years, she had become even more resilient— never wanting to give up.

She had immense faith in her calling as an educator and decided to get working on building a school in Kolkata. Her passion for educating children pushed her to go door-to-door, to ask parents to send their children to her makeshift school, near the refugee area in Jadavpur.

After noticing the rising interest in parents to provide an education for their children, Monu was able to set up a second school for kids, near Santoshpur.

The partition that ripped many families apart, was strangely instrumental in bringing some long-lost relatives together. Monu Rani, who had lost her family

145

while she was on the other side of the border, was reunited with her siblings' families, as every refugee tried to find those common threads that could sew the torn tapestry of their families once again.

She never remarried or adopted another child, but would spoil her grand nieces and nephews silly.

The school continued to be led by her until 1989, when she breathed her last at the age of 87 having lived a long and strangely fulfilled life. With no heir to take her legacy forward, the school closed with her passing, but what remained as fond memories of her legacy were her will to survive, and her resilient spirit to make something meaningful out of her life.

'She never needed a conventional family structure to shower her love', said my mother, one of the grandchildren of Monu Rani's elder sister, while narrating the life of her dear Monuma. 'She would always come with something for us in her *baalti-bag*. If we ever complained about studying, Monuma would say – education will equip you to handle difficult situations in life. Never turn away from it!'

Glossary:

Uthon: an open courtyard in the center of traditional homes
Baba: Father
Maa: Mother
Bornomala: Bengali alphabets
Kaash phool: Also called wild sugarcane, it is a form of grass native to Indian subcontinent
Kaku: Uncle
Master-moshai: teacher
Uludhoni: A sound uttered by women in certain parts of India during festive occasions
Shonkho: Conch shell
Baalti-bag: An old style of bag resembling a small bucket

Phula

Shweta Ghosh, India

It was a bright and beautiful dawn in my quiet and peaceful village of Bahadurpur, a village in the hinterlands of Purnia; a small town of North Bihar. The

149

young Sun with a few aimlessly floating cotton clouds formed a backdrop in the lurid blue sky, promising a hot day.

Far amidst the maze of vast lush green paddy fields a tall slim figure walks, nimbly balancing an earthen pitcher on her head. Her form is blurred by the heat haze. Occasionally she wipes her head with the end of her scarf. Slowly the figure becomes clear. She has a dusky complexion and a lissom full body with grace that is rare for a village belle. She is Phula, Ramkripal and Kinnar's only daughter.

Phula passes without noticing me.

'*Mai O mai*, I have fetched the water,' Phula calls out to her mother as she lowers the pots on the neat mud and cow dung plastered courtyard. The walls were beautifully painted with various forms of human figurines in white; mostly done by Kinnar with Phula's help; a rural art.

'I am leaving for school,' Phula calls out.

'*Aree ruk ja lado*, here, take the roti. You won't return before dusk I know,' Kinnar had to stoop low to come out the small door, adjusting her *pallu* over her head.

'Oh Mai I am not hungry, and if I am, then there is always the Mahajan's field with its juicy sugarcane to chew on,' Phula replied mischievously, eyes wide and shining, lips twisted in a naughty smile. The look that helped Phula get away with her mischief; a perpetual half

150

merry and half absent minded smile that had the power to soften the cruellest of hearts.

'*Haye ram*! Don't you dare enter the Mahajan's field,' Kinnar called out in despair as Phula ran out of the courtyard picking up her *jhola*.

Both Ramkripal and Kinnar were illiterate. Ramkripal worked at Lala's shop while Kinnar was Lala's house maid. They had a patch of land where they grew vegetables.

I am Shweta and I hail from one of those fast-developing urban cities of India, where it is fashionable to be working 'on rural developments,' or 'running an NGO'. Frankly, bitten by the same bug, I ended up in Bahadurpur, and got seriously involved in a literacy mission. With my father's surplus supply of money, effective influence, laced with my stubbornness to boost it, I started a school in this area. And here I am, into my third year and well settled. After the initial rejection, I have been accepted, respected and also loved.

This is where I met Phula, a happy, beautiful and strong-willed girl of thirteen. I was astounded by her intelligent mind. She was very good with numbers and memory. As she started coming to the school along with a handful of reluctant children, I found her to be extremely focused and hard-working. Her encouraging parents took delight in her studies, a rarity in such rural belts of Bihar.

'And why not Didiji,' shyly confessed Kinnar one evening over *bajra roti* and *chai*, Ramji blessed us with

151

her after five years after our marriage, Phula's father was about to remarry when she happened!'

I was not amused.

Life was peaceful till Ramkripal was being craftily reminded in *Chaupal*, that a girl should be married off before she attains her puberty otherwise 'they' go astray and Phula, was past that age at fifteen! Phula, on the other hand, was determined to continue with her studies. I wanted her to complete her 10th grade and so did Kinner. Ramkripal was under pressure.

It was in between such tumults that Bhairon Ram, Phula's uncle, brought this particular marriage alliance.

'Bhauji, the boy is intermediate pass, and will surely get a peon's job in some office. They have promised to let Phula continue with her studies. She will live in the town and have better prospects. Where will you get such a good alliance?' Bhairon countered Kinnar upon sensing her dilemma.

'What about their demand for *dahej*?' hesitantly, a quietly sitting Ramkripal asked.

'Nothing much,' Bhairon waved his hands down-playing the most pertinent and difficult question. 'The boy has to walk a long distance for his college, so a cycle will be all and you don't want your only son-in- law to go without a watch and gold chain or do you?' he looked from the corner of his eyes.

'*Bas*, rest whatever jewellery, clothes and gifts you intend to gift is your decision. They will not voice their demand. Such progressive people...' deviously everything was said.

Concern playing upon his face, Ramkripal watched the evening sky with a *bidi* in his hand. The crackling of the *chullha* spoke of the tension with sparks flying through the smoke. Kinnar indignantly kneaded the dough.

After a lot of persuasion, a despondent Phula acquiesced in her parent's decision.

One night as we lay on our *charpoys*, under the open sky of the courtyard, Phula spoke to me in a faraway voice, Didi, I agreed to the alliance because they will let me continue with my studies. I too will be a *sheharwali* like Gulabbo.' A tinkle of laughter followed. I turned to look at her smiling face gazing at a billion sparkling stars, synonymous with the dreams in her eyes. I was happy for this moment and worried for the future.

Thus, Phula stepped out of her cocoon into an unknown life and territory far away from us. I presented her husband with the much-demanded bicycle. Ramkripal had to mortgage his piece of land and was in considerable debt. Smeared in orange vermillion, wrists laden with red tinkling glass bangles and a deprecatory smile, Phula left for her *sasural* accompanied *with* her meek looking boy of a husband. I was hopeful that her aspirations would not be nipped in the bud.

The village was emptied of its charm without Phula. I occasionally met her parents breaking their backs

153

in the field to pay off the debts and got to know about her well-being. I felt happy for her and rebuked myself for my negative thoughts.

Months passed. One day an overjoyed Kinnar informed me of Phula's pregnancy! I feigned joy but was appalled. Pregnant at sixteen! Ramkripal had gone to bring her home for the birth.

I looked forward to her arrival but when she came, it was a different Phula. The lively girl was gone. Those eyes that shone with liquid brilliance, dancing, expressing on behalf of her lips, in their place were lacklustre orbs sunken with fatigue. Vacant eyes that beheld nothing. She spent most of her time with me. I tried to cheer her up, read to her about health and hygiene, explained things pertaining to pregnancy and childbirth which are alien in these fringes of our society. Phula listened to them attentively.

'I miss my home, the fragrance of the summer flowers in my courtyard, the silence of the winter nights and dew drenched mornings…' her voice trailed. Slowly she started talking.

'Didiji, my in-laws enrolled me in a school but I was seldom allowed to attend. My husband is a spineless man and never stood up for me. In fact, he fled some two months ago and I have not seen him ever since,' her eyes welled up.

'They have threatened not to take me back if I divulge any of this to my parents. School is a distant dream now.' Phula broke down.

154

I couldn't believe my ears. In between hiccups and tears, Phula continued with her heartbreaking tale. 'They called me characterless for talking and helping my fifteen-year-old brother-in-law with his lessons! I was beaten mercilessly as I tried to call you once from a telephone booth.' Stunned and infuriated beyond words I held her shuddering frail body on my lap letting her cry and pour her heart out. I promised myself and her that I will take care of her.

But first the pregnancy had to be handled. In due course Phula mothered a beautiful girl, Shaila. A deliriously happy Phula seemed to have forgotten her problems temporarily. She was weaving dreams around her child. Her in-laws never came to see their granddaughter, for them, this little girl was a burden, an unwanted girl child.

I persuade Ramkripal to talk to Phula's in-laws and reason it out with them. He refused, citing that Phula is their *bahu* now, so they get to decide about her. His interference may backfire and they may disown her, leaving them disgraced.

'I am already neck deep into debt; how will I feed two extra mouths? Please don't put all this into her head Didiji. Let her find her happiness and come to terms with her fate.' He pleaded with me. I was disappointed and immensely troubled by Ramkripal's words. It was not entirely his fault, the community he lived within had shaped his thoughts, controlled his actions and he couldn't ignore them. It required a strong mind, which he evidently lacked.

155

I had to leave Bahadurpur on some pretext and at the time was unaware of the lifelong consequences my absence would bring.

Since no one came from Phula's in-law's place to take her back, Ramkripal, I was told, had gone to drop Phula with a twenty-day old Shaila in her arms.

A week later, I received a frantic call from Phula. She was hysterical. 'Didi they are planning to kill Shaila, they will kill my baby! I overheard them discussing stuffing her tiny mouth with salt or paddy grains, or worse, they might even take her and dump her somewhere. Time is running out Didiji... please take me home.

I tried to tell her to be safe till I arrive in a day's time. But she didn't listen and kept crying over the phone.

'She is all I have, Didiji. Imagine her face enriched with an innocent smile, her tender lips tugging at my bosom, how can I see her die? I am helpless Didiji, please take me home...'

Before I could say anything, the line disconnected. I kept calling the number to no avail. The very next evening I left for Purnia with a scared and shaken Ramkripal. This time I was unwavering and adamant about bringing her back for good.

We reached her in-law's place with the local police, anticipating resistance and unaware of the dreadful and shocking news that was waiting for us.

'Phula', shrieked her shrewd mother-in-law, 'has run off with someone along with that witch of a child, bringing shame upon us!' We stood there numbed and traumatized, unable to comprehend the situation.

Upon interrogation she handed us a piece of crumpled paper. The anguish and the pain in those words hit me hard. Helplessness screamed at me in those seven words. Ramkripal sobbed silently crouching on the floor.

It read, '*Didiji, kash Bapu bhi yahin sochen hotein.*'

I launched a massive hunt but all met with a dead-end.

Part 2

Nineteen years have passed since that fateful day but not a single day without remembering Phula and her fate.

Today as I was crossing the crowded Dak-Bunglow road I was stamped on my foot. I winced and looked up to face a young girl apologetically smiling at me.

'I am so sorry Didi, the puddle of water made me jump and land at your feet. Please forgive me. Sorry, I am actually late for my class,' with that she vanished.

I was disturbed by the familiarity of the face. It haunted me, the uncanny resemblance. The next day I found myself on the same road, fingers crossed.

157

Yes, there she was! Walking toward me, her face became anxious as she saw me, anticipating an earful for the puddle jumping fiasco the day before.

'I am sorry, please don't', she began.

Me, 'what's your name?'

'Shalini Kumari.'

'And…and you Mother's?'

'Phulwanti, but why are you asking? Didi please don't…'

I was already pulling her by her elbow toward a vacant rickshaw.

'Take me to your home.'

Was Shaila, Shalini? It was a ten-minute ride in complete silence. My hopes gave away as we stopped outside a big beautiful house. Shalini took me inside. 'Maa someone insists on meeting you.' Shalini called out as we entered the plush living room, my heart pounding. 'Who Shailu?' Phula came out of the room! She stood rooted looking at me in disbelief.

'Didi, you took a long time to find me. I waited for you all through,' she threw herself in my arms sobbing.

Phula after sensing the plot to be set on fire along with her daughter had fled the house and boarded a bus to Patna with little money that she had.

158

A labourer woman gave her shelter upon seeing her alone and vulnerable with an infant. Phula's appearance, her ability to read and write helped her get a job at this very house. The lady after hearing her story tried to connect Phula with her parents, which she refused. Phula didn't want to go back to her life of oppression and wanted to give life another shot; A life where she could take her own decisions and make her own choices. She had already taken the first step when she had to flee her in-laws place with her infant daughter. Escaping death, that very moment had she realised that she wished to live, to fight and not resign to fate.

A seventeen-year-old *woman* made that resolution. And as life would have played out, she stayed back with this kind lady under her love and care. With time, Phula became their trusted house keeper.

Phula took it upon herself to educate Shaila, a dream that she couldn't fulfill for herself. Shaila, was now a young lady in college. The pride in Phula's eye was well deserved.

'Didiji every day I thought of you and your teachings. I tried to adhere to them in my everyday life and carried on…'

My memory meandered to that quaint village of Bahadurpur, its lush green fields, the huge banyan tree with charpoys below its shaded canopy, the narrow lanes of the mud and lime plastered huts with thatched roofs, lazy hot afternoons of a scorching summer, still winter nights and my chit chats with Phula as the warmth of the *angithe*e engulfed us.

159

Life had been bitter for Phula but rewarded with Shaila, it is sweet enough to sustain her for her future. I looked at her and my heart swelled with love. A fighter never gives up. We had come a long way.

Glossary:

Chai: tea
Chullha: earthen stove
Chaupal: village meeting place usually for men
Didi: elder sister
Dahej: dowry
Haye ram; oh lord
Kash Bapu bhi yahi sochein hoten: I wish father thought on the sameline
Jhola: cloth bag
Mai: mother
Mahajan: money lender
Pallu: one end of the sari that hangs from the shoulder
Ruk jaa: wait
Sheharwali: town girl
Sasural: in law's place

The journey continues for many ....

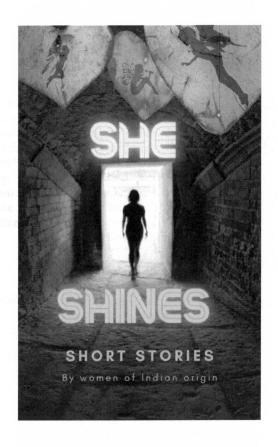

Authors Profile

Abhilasha Kumar, Switzerland *(Editor)*

Abhilasha Kumar is a researcher with a keen interest in a myriad spectrum of subjects, including astronomy, unified physics, biology, nature, wildlife and its conservation. She is currently based in Basel, Switzerland working in medical commu-nication, and is mother to two young boys and a very pampered canine. Exploring the inner and outer worlds, Abhilasha enjoys traveling to diverse places and delves in spiritual practices to discover inner realms. Previously, she was contributing author in the anthologies She Speaks and She Celebrates. Abhilasha is a contributing editor and author of three short stories in 'She Reflects'.

Ashwathy Menon, India *(Production)*

Ashwathy started her career in Sales and Marketing functions besides being involved in various Training inter-ventions. Her diverse experiences in Corporate and Academia evolved her into a disciplined person. She found her mojo in Arts during her sabbatical, post motherhood. Now a full-time Artist, curating her works under the '*huesbyashwathy*' brand, Ashwathy is a Writer by interest. She channelises her thoughts and expressions through paints and words. The last couple of years saw her writing works published in multiple anthologies. When at leisure, she is immersed in a book or is singing her heart out. Ashwathy lives in Mumbai with her husband and daughter.

Anamika, Australia

Anamika is the nom de plume adopted by the writer of this short story. She wears many hats – NGO executive, banker, academic and business owner – but is proudest of her role as the mother of two boys. Anamika loves music, keeping fit and travelling, and hopes to keep sharing her experiences by finding the time to keep up with her writing.

Bidisha Chakraborti, US

Bidisha is a professional specialized in the Insurance industry for a large consulting firm. Born in a Bengali family, brought up in Chandigarh and married to a Tamilian, blended cultures (and kitchens!) make her feel at home. Outside of her day job as a researcher, she likes to find time to travel with her husband. Despite being a novice storyteller, her interest in writing comes from middle school days where two of her closest friends had encouraged her to 'put pen to her thoughts'. Bidisha is currently residing in the Greater New York area with her husband.

Brindarica Bose, Switzerland *(Publisher)*

Brindarica Bose, studied science, business administration and fine arts. She is an artist and works part-time as an art teacher in an art school, and as a Publications Manager in an international association. She lives in Switzerland with her family and founded Bose Creative Publishers in 2020, which is a collaborative publishing platform. She published her first book of short stories 'Swiss Masala' in 2018, and thereafter contributed to the SHE anthologies. IG @brindaricabose @bosecreativepublishers

Ekta Sharma, Australia *(Chief Coordinator, 2022)*

Born in India, Ekta received B.Sc degree in Mathematical Sciences, M.Sc in Operational research and M.Phil degree from University of Delhi, India. Her current research is in artificial intelligence at a University in Australia. Her research work has received funding from the Australian Defence Science and Technology Group, the Australian Institute of Mathematical Sciences, and the Australian Government. Writing has been her all-time ambition and love, and her proficiency in nine languages or metalinguistic awareness helps her to connect with a broader range of people. She regularly publishes research articles, books and now foraying into Hindi and English poems. She believes that writing is an efficient means for expressing emotions. She hopes her stories will be like a warm winter hug for the readers, a soft shoulder squeeze, that will tug at your heartstrings when you need them the most.

Jesleen Gill Papneja, USA *(Coordinator 2022)*

Jesleen lives in Virginia, U.S with her husband and two children. A dentist and consultant by profession, Jesleen is a red wine and champagne enthusiast. She is an ardent reader who loves to read all genres from Enid Blyton to Khalil Gibran. Theater is her undying passion and she has also been a Bollywood dance instructor. More spiritual than religious,

Jesleen loves life and lives by the mantra, "life is too short for unfinished business – when there is a lesson to be learned, learn it and move on."

Nandini Sircar Nandi, UAE

Nandini has extensive experience as a television, radio and print journalist in India and the UAE. She currently works as a Correspondent with Dubai's oldest national daily, *Khaleej Times.* Her reportage also includes broadcast journalism with associations like NDTV and TV18 network. She was Emirate's morning voice as a radio news presenter during her tenure at the Arabian Radio Network (ARN). Nandini is a news buff, a music lover, driven by wanderlust and enjoys reading, writing narrating stories, cooking and driving. A mother to a four-year-old, she is always on her toes. Nandini believes that, "Victory belongs to the most persevering."

Rejina Sadhu, Switzerland (*Editor*)

Dr. Rejina Sadhu is a neurobiologist turned regulatory medical writer who finds the world of written words fascinating and explores it with her two children. A Malayali born in Mumbai, she moved to Switzerland for her PhD, got married to a Bengali and continued to explore the world through books, travel, music and food. She started writing poems and stories at a young age for her school magazine, and moved on to publish in university publications. The organizers of the Bombay Hindi Sahitya Parishad published her Hindi poems. Her scientific essays earned critical acclaim from the Nobel Laureate Harold Kroto.

Raka Mitra, Netherlands *(Editor)*

Raka Mitra was born in India and since then has grown up across 3 continents, India, Africa and Australia. She now calls the Netherlands home where she lives with her husband and young daughter. She hasn't yet won any awards but keeps on day-dreaming about this, almost as often she dreams of blue skies and warm sun on grey Dutch winters.

Saleha Singh, Australia

Saleha Singh is a Publication Lead for a non-profit organisation in Melbourne. She lives with her husband, two daughters and three dogs. A passionate community worker, she is the founder of a bi-weekly webcast – *Chai, Chat & Community* – which discusses overlooked South Asian issues. She is the President of IndianCare, a not-for-profit organisation that looks after the welfare needs of vulnerable Indians in Melbourne. Her other pro-bono work is a Director of PeaceMeals that connects refugees and asylum seekers to established Australians over a plate of food. More: https://wordpalette.com.au/

Savvy Soumya Misra, India

Savvy Soumya Misra believes that stories of people and communities on the margins need to be heard. These stories often end up in studies or research papers drowned in jargons. Her attempt is to reach out to readers like herself - the layperson. Born in Jamshedpur, she

167

now lives in Noida with her best friend (and husband) Udit. Savvy is a huge fan of the 90's Bollywood music, is crazy about lamps, loves food, is on the lookout for a good thriller, and is an occasional knitter.

Shweta Dasgupta Ghosh, India

Shweta Dasgupta has freelanced for many years in leading newspapers like Hidustan Times, Times of India and The Indian Nation. She writes in English, Hindi and Bangla. Her short stories have been published earlier. Nowadays she juggles between being a mom, daughter and a wife. Shweta is passionate about writing, pens poems, short stories and shayeries. She likes to express herself in this way. 'Every Writer has this deep-down desire to be read, appreciated and be accepted by his/her reader and she is no exception to this.' Shweta adds. She lives in the City of Joy, Kolkata, with her teenage daughter, a son (four-legged Joe) and her mother.

Teesta Ghosh, USA (*Editor, Proofreader*)

Teesta is an academic by profession who lives with her family in the Washington, DC area. She led an itinerant life living in different parts of India in her childhood and considers that experience to be profoundly influential in shaping her world view. Subsequently she moved to the US to pursue her doctoral studies. Outside the classroom, she has been a manager for her son's soccer team, judged debate competitions and was a member of a book club devoted to child pedagogy. She enjoys traveling, is a nature enthusiast, loves to cook and

168

considers herself a writer by accident rather than design. She abides by the motto; "be human, be humane."

Thangam Pillai, India

Thangam writes because she cannot help it! Neck deep into the world of educational product and infrastructure, writing is her stress buster. Recently however she is bitten by the publishing bug and here she presents her attempts to you all. 'Kruthe Prathikruthe', and 'Auto Maintenance Industry: An Insight' are two of her e-published work. Short stories and poetries churn out whenever life experiences mill through the whirlpool of emotions. For more of her dishes visit http://5ea5201043b1b.site123.me/ or simply google Tang's Corner site 123.

....

Thank you for reading this book and helping us in the 'Books for a Cause' project. Please post your review in Amazon and other portals, and recommend this book to your friends and family.

Proceedings from SHE books sales are donated to various charitable institutions. Editors, authors, publisher volunteer their time and expertise to tell stories, and run the 'SHE' books project, to give a creative platform to voices less heard. By reading this book, you are contributing to this good cause. Refer to other books published by the SHE group of writers: She Speaks (2019), She Celebrates (2021), She Reflects (2021), available in amazon.

169

BOSE CREATIVE PUBLISHERS

www.bosecreativepublishers.ch

Bose Creative Publishers, established in 2020 in Switzerland is a collaborative publishing company whose aim is to encourage writers and artists, to publish a book together. Books Published till March 2022 (QR code above):

1. Sketching Diaries, 2020
2. Social Entrepreneurs and Change Makers, 2020
3. She Reflects, 2021
4. Indian Grandmas Secret Recipes, 2021
5. Emotions in Rhythm, 2021
6. She Celebrates, 2021
7. In Search of Sherpur: An Immigrant's Memoir, 2021
8. She Shines, 2022.